I0818068

A Beaumont Bros Circus Mystery #2

THE DETECTIVE'S NIGHTMARE

TABI SLICK

This is a work of fiction. Names, characters, places, events, and incidents are either products of the author's imagination or are used fictitiously. Any resemblance to persons living or dead is entirely coincidental and not intended by the author.

Published by SWC Indie Press

www.SWCIndiePress.com

Hard Cover Edition, 2022

ISBN: 978-1-7345568-7-2

Printed in the United States of America

www.TabiSlick.com

Created with Vellum

TRANSITIONED UNIVERSE BOOKS BY TABI SLICK

Tompkin's School: For The Extraordinarily Talented
Tompkin's School: For The Dearly Departed
Tompkin's School: For The Resurrected

~

The Unforgivable Act
The Detective's Nightmare
The Yuletide Killer

~

Timur's Escape

To stay in the know about upcoming series visit:
www.tabislick.com/join

To my parents, Lonnie and Sarah.
For instilling in me a passion for reading.

You're a man haunted by those two most terrible words: What if?

— ÜBER-MORLOCK, *THE TIME MACHINE*

CONTENTS

HALIFAX FANTASY MAP

1

ONLY ON BRUNSWICK STREET

Halifax, Nova Scotia

Barnaby rushed down the dark, wet cobblestones. His uneven gasps billowed white smoke behind him as he raced against the bitter wind. The lively echoes from a pub just ahead beckoned him, the twinkling lamps flickering as he made haste. Glancing over his shoulder at the foreboding night, he ducked hastily into the Two Crows.

"Back so soon, eh?" The barkeep grinned from behind the long wooden bar.

"It's gotten bad out there," he mumbled, ignoring the barkeeper's patronising taunt. He didn't care that this would be the second time here that night. He wasn't about to go back out after what he'd just heard in the wind. The tin flute called, heralding some unknown danger nearing and he wouldn't take the chance of being caught outdoors.

Rubbing the sudden knot in his neck, he ambled his aching body to a seat at the bar. He jumped when the door clanged behind him. With a quick check from his peripheral, he let out a sigh of relief that it was only a patron staggering on his way out.

"Gin," Barnaby ordered, barely looking up to notice the barkeeper staring at him from behind raised eyebrows and a smirk upon his lips.

"What's with you tonight?" the burly man jeered. "You look like you've just been to Deadman's Island."

"If only." Barnaby squeezed his eyes shut, hoping he could get the ringing from his ear. He hoped it wasn't what he suspected. "Do you hear that?"

The barkeeper frowned. "Are you sure you want another?"

Barnaby's thick hand slammed against the gleaming maple. "I swear, Tom, after that case I did for you, I think I've earned another. On the house."

A few droopy-eyed patrons glanced their way briefly before returning to their conversations, quickly lost in their own fit of giggles.

Tom's lip twitched at the reference to catching his dame chatting up a fellow outside of the officers' quarters. He fumbled around the small space behind the bar, fetching the gin and a fresh glass.

Barnaby gripped his chest, his heart racing at the anticipation of something terrible nearing. What would it be this time? He shivered as he thought about the many unknowns. There was nothing he could do except to wait and see what happened. Taking deep, calming breaths, he shook his racing mind. It was impossible to hear what he'd heard. No one had been around. He'd checked to be sure of it. Still, the shrill notes of a tine flute resonated on the wind like a haunting caw of a harbour seagull. It was a sound that haunted him ever since he'd found the first one, not two weeks before when he'd witnessed the impossible.

Dozens of ducks—nay—hundreds of them marched in a

single-file line down from the Citadel. No one could explain where they'd come from or why yet on they marched, defying all reason, down the muddy streets before diving into the Halifax Harbour. They dove deep into the water, each one drowning themselves. As the city's only private detective, the citizens looked to him to explain all of it. Why they thought he could decipher something like that he had no idea. He never worked on cases involving death. He couldn't stomach the stench of rot and decay. Perhaps they figured this restriction didn't apply to animals.

Regardless, this phenomenon was beyond him. He couldn't figure out what had caused the ducks to do such a horrific thing. To his knowledge, ducks only committed suicide when being hunted and no one would hunt in such a public area. It was forbidden.

The only clue he'd been left with was the necklace each duck pulled from the water wore. A rectangular box not much larger than a pocket watch hung on each chain around their necks.

He wished he'd never opened the first one. That's when the music began, an ominous warning before something dreadfully horrid happened. It wasn't just the music that haunted him most, but what he found in each box. A small, velvet pouch filled with rotten teeth, caked with blood and grime. He'd kept them all as a clue, though they didn't provide much. No matter how many times he inspected them and tried to make sense of it, he found himself plunging deeper into a state of madness. Food lost its tastiness, sleep lost its restfulness, and his mind couldn't stop obsessing over what unimaginable darkness could've caused all of this to happen.

However, it didn't end with the ducks. Oh, how he wished that had been the end of it. Fate had to call him to a disturbance at Hazel Tilcott's home. Her precious cat had its entire liver pulled through its oesophagus. It was then he'd heard the tin flute again, that horrible thrumming that kept him up at all hours of the night warning him something terrible was about to take place yet again.

He found the customary box stuffed within the dislodged organ. It had required all of Barnaby's might not to faint on the spot. His stomach naturally queasy, he much preferred solving petty thefts or missing persons. Anything less gruesome and impossible. Who would do such a thing to a cat?

Stranger and stranger events filled his days and with them brought the melancholic tune of the tin flute, teetering between a pleasant minor to a jolting sharp always on the verge of a crescendo and another bag of teeth. Then there was the terrible event that had brought Barnaby to the pub to drown himself in gin.

24 Hours Earlier

It was a brisk winter evening with the promise of a storm on the horizon. Barnaby pulled at his wool jacket, wishing he'd worn his warmer sack coat as he marched across the timbers of Fairbanks Wharf. Excitement swept through him bringing a youthful spring to his ageing step. Though he was not yet greying, the lines above his brow hinted that his wavy umber hair parted down the middle would soon be peppered with it.

"G' mornin', Detective Grey." The dockmaster tipped his hat.

"Mr Dods. Any new break-ins this week?"

"Not this week. Although, not sure why anyone would

want to sneak into my warehouse. It's not like I'm a privateer."

The much older man's belly shook with laughter, the buttons on his vest nearly popping out.

Barnaby smiled, the corners of his eyes crinkling. "Probably just children playing a prank, I'm sure."

"Yes, indeed." The dockmaster took a puff of his pipe, eyeing Barnaby through the smoke. "So what brings ye down to Lower Water again? I can't imagine there being more ducks."

"No, nothing of that sort." His stomach quivered at the mention of the drowning ducks. "I'm expecting the *Augustus*."

Mr Dods nodded. "The merchantman should be arriving here any minute. What's it to you?"

"My nephew's come to visit his old uncle." Barnaby lifted his chin up in pride. "He wants to get into the detective business and so I plan to show him the ropes. I guess you could call him my protégé."

He'd never had any children of his own and considered Archie the closest thing to a son. Archie was the most observant child he'd ever met, and now that he was older, he'd been showing an interest in Barnaby's profession, much to his father's disapproval. Barnaby's little sister had married a doctor. Not a bad profession, just not one he'd considered a good fit for Archie, who'd taken after his uncle's squeamish nature.

"Ah." The dockmaster took another draw of his pipe.

"I've never stayed in one place so long to have the luxury, but I daresay Halifax has had its way with me."

"And happy we are to—"

A thud shook the floorboards of the dock as several crates toppled over despite one of the nearby dock labourer's desperate attempts to keep them upright.

"OY! What you think you're doin'?" Mr Dods's gruff baritone startled the young lad. "Clean that up and get it packed in the sheds before I find ten more o' ye to replace you."

The dockmaster shook his head, turning back to Barnaby, who was checking his pocket watch for the umpteenth time. "Have a new docker, I see."

"Yeah, the kid's only been here a few months. Living at the Poor House Cemetery and came begging me for a job. Felt bad for him, being so fresh from across the pond and all."

"You've such a kind heart." Barnaby clicked his pocket watch closed and tucked it into his pocket. He stopped when he caught the eye of the second dock labourer, the likes of which he'd not seen since his escapades through the Ottoman lands. The memory of Turkish Delight made his mouth water.

The dark man wearing an unusual sash tied around his waist was helping a younger lad carry the crates portside, smirking at Barnaby when they passed them by and making Barnaby double-take. "What's his name?"

"John. John Walsh, I think it is." Mr Dods motioned towards the younger, dishevelled docker.

"No, the man there with him."

"Hmm?" Mr Dods glanced over his shoulder before looking quizzically back at Barnaby. "There's only just the one John."

"Not John, the other"—Barnaby stopped when he looked back only to see one dock labourer. A much smaller young man wearing a ruddy cloth cap. The Turkish man had seemingly vanished into thin air—"one."

Barnaby glanced up and down the dock, searching for the foreigner. He was nowhere to be seen, somehow vanishing into thin air. Placing his hands on his hips, he could've sworn there was another docker. Perhaps he'd been mistaken? He hadn't eaten his supper yet, and it had been a quite long day.

Perhaps he was just a bit lightheaded. Yes, that must've been it.

Returning his focus to the sea, the timber groaned as Barnaby neared the dock's edge, peering across the gentle water of the Halifax Harbour. Seagulls glided, circling about George Island and the stone walls of Fort Charlotte barely visible in the darkening sky.

"Storm shouldn't reach us until after nightfall," Mr Dods called, heading back down the dock. "Should give ye plenty of time."

With a harrumph, Barnaby wished Mr Dods a good evening just as a fog curled around his ankles, obscuring the rustling blue waters. The hairs on his forearms stood upright as unnatural electricity rushed through the wind.

Barnaby pulled at his handkerchief, dabbing the mist from his forehead that the sudden gust brought as he studied the expanding harbour just beyond the Royal Engineers Yard.

The ocean darkened against the white frothing waves which crashed against each other. The angry waters splashed onto the bank just below the brick Gas Works plant on the edge of the Royal Engineers Wharf. The once gentle blue waters swirled like a menacing snake.

Barnaby blinked rapidly, trying with all of his might not to tip over. Shielding his eyes with his forearm, all the colour drained from his face when a lightning bolt as violet as his patterned waistcoat slashed into one of the five masts of the *Augustus* bobbing just behind the Gas Works building.

"Dear Lord!" Barnaby trembled, running down the dock towards the port now emptying as sailors found shelter from the sudden storm.

It wasn't just a storm, at least not one Barnaby had ever seen in his life. He pushed past Mr Dods, who called after him, but he couldn't hear the old man over the howling wind.

Barnaby's chest ached as he pushed himself to a full sprint from Fairbanks Wharf down the path towards the Royal Engineers Wharf now being pummeled by the rising seawater.

Just as he reached the dock stretching past the Gas Works building, another bright light of now purple flashed from the sky striking the water sending it churning into the side of the *Augustus*. The vessel swayed, the side crashing into the Gas Works building sending wood splintering in every direction.

Barnaby squeezed his eyes shut, the sound of another otherwordly lightning bolt flashing across the harbour dulled by the faint hum of a tin flute.

"Please, don't hurt my nephew," Barnaby sobbed, the ominous music leaving him crippled with fear.

Metal screeched as the sudden heat cut into the bitter cold. Barnaby blinked, catching the black smoke as it curled from the fire that now engulfed the plant.

The water flashed blood red, the churning waters forcing the ship to go faster than Barnaby had ever witnessed a merchant ship go. Men aboard clamoured to slow the ship down, but the harbour had another idea. The ship teetered back and forth, its scorched side taking in water as it barreled past the destroyed Gas Works building towards the Royal Engineers Wharf.

"It's not going to make it," Barnaby cried, racing back towards Lower Water Street where dockers and merchants stood, gaping at the violet typhoon forming in the skies above.

His breath heaved, nearing the Royal Engineers Wharf where the *Augustus* threatened to meet its final resting place.

"BARNABY! RUN!" Mr Dods shouted.

It was no use. Nothing could deter Barnaby now. The waters swirled clockwise, bringing the ship above sea level. The vessel fought to stay topside, but another snap of purple and violet lightning broke through the funnel threatening to engulf the *Augustus* just as the wave spewed its crimson waters onto the shore, sending the ship tearing through the royal dock.

With the cries of the survivors on the wind drowning out the tin flute, Barnaby ran for the fluttering masts.

Men in torn uniforms picked themselves up from the rubble. The belly of the ship had been ripped to shreds and those who survived flung their limbs over anything that would support them, treading their way to safety.

"Archie!" Barnaby shaded his eyes from the rain sprinkling down upon the mess, the waves receding as quickly as they'd materialised and with it, the mystical colours vanished from the water as it returned to a normal deep blue-grey.

The vein in Barnaby's neck stood out, pulsating rapidly with his racing heart. He scanned the survivors being helped from the icy water. Mr Dods extended a helping hand to a young woman with no hat, but piles of snow-white hair pinned in curls on top of her head. It was much too white for her age, Barnaby thought. A few other men followed not too far behind along with a girl with the brightest red mane he'd ever seen in his life. None of them was his nephew. Where could he be?

Then he spotted it. A body hunched against a broken piece of the side of the ship, rocking against the waters. Barnaby rushed in, nearly slipping on the rocky ocean surface. He reached for the body's side, turning it carefully. His eyes were met with the ashen face of his nephew, a cut dripping from his greying lips. A sudden weakness sent Barnaby falling to his knees in the ankle-deep water.

"Archie." Barnaby's hands shook, gripping the boy's shoulders and lowering his ear checking for a pulse. There was none. "My dear boy," he sobbed, tears spilling onto his cheek.

A tinge of pain hit his gut and he gasped for air. How could this happen? What kind of evil brought violet lightning, turning the water from its natural blue to blood red? What devil angered Poseidon to make the waves send the *Augustus* tumbling into the Halifax Harbour? And why had it taken his nephew from him? His chest heaved against his sobs, his cries blending with the commotion from the port.

What seemed like hours, were just mere minutes. When Barnaby's tears dried, he noticed peculiar marks around his nephew's neck. Deep black and blue contusions marked the boy's throat. He inhaled quickly, his stomach quivering as he moved to get a closer look. Under further examination, the bruises resembled handprints and the larynx had definitely been crushed. He swayed, suddenly feeling faint. Was it possible the unnatural storm hadn't been his nephew's cause of death? Could it have been… murder? He swallowed hard when the words formed in his mind.

Then, something caught his eye just under the surface of the water beside the body. Barnaby expelled the breath he held, shoving his hand into the freezing water. Beads of rain mixed with his own tears as he pulled a silver chain out, bringing with it the white knuckles of his nephew who clung to it as if his life had depended on it.

Barnaby squeezed his eyes closed, praying this wasn't what he thought it was. Dread mixed with nausea filled him as he pried Archie's stone-cold fingers open. A shudder ran through his body when he laid eyes on the small, rectangular box in his nephew's hand. From the rusted metal encasing to the strange, interlocking pyramid symbols on the lid, it appeared to be identical to the others. Unfortunately, there was only one way to be sure.

Carefully pushing against the latch, he gritted his teeth as the sharp corners pressed against his wet palm. With one last heave, the lid flipped open. Whispers surrounded Barnaby, stirring the wind around him nearly knocking the box from his hands. Through the gust of wind, the voices faded into a single melodic tune of the tin flute.

Barnaby's ears rang, standing up onto shaky feet, his feeble muscles straining against his skin as a rage he'd never felt before soared through him. He chucked the box as far out into the harbour as he could manage. He didn't even bother looking into the pouch it contained. He knew it would contain yet another bag of teeth. Only this time the bag of teeth was found on the body of his dead nephew and the thought of anyone hurting Archie made him want to vomit. And then it made him want to drink.

The Two Crows, Halifax

THE CLINK of a glass jolted Barnaby from his dreadful memory, the clear liquid sloshing from the glass of gin Tom set in front of him.

"On the house," Tom said, mockingly.

Barnaby rubbed his weary eyes, bringing the glass up to his lips.

CRACK!

Pieces of reflecting glass flew everywhere as all of the glass in sight shattered into jagged pieces, blanketing the pub. Women screamed and men stumbled over themselves trying to figure out the source of the commotion.

A thud against the door to the establishment made everyone who heard it freeze, Barnaby included. His heart pounded as he placed his broken gin glass down. The cuts on his fingers stung as the contents of his unfinished drink spilt down his hand and onto the bar.

The barstool groaned as he slid from it, ambling past the shaken patrons. All eyes were on him, their expectant expressions sending the message clear that it was up to him to see what was causing all of this commotion. He was getting tired of being the town's only detective. Now he understood why his colleague Davies, though many years his junior, was already in retirement. Barnaby was getting much too old for this and he wasn't sure his heart could take much more.

His hand shook as he reached for the door, taking a brief pause before swinging it to the side.

Crows flapped their feathery wings in his face as a flock flew inside, their mission to come indoors defying all logic.

When the last of the birds fluttered past him into the pub, it was the body hanging just beyond the door that made Barnaby take pause.

"Everyone, stay inside!" He ordered, pushing himself into the cold night's breeze and shutting the door into the pub behind him. He stepped out onto the sidewalk, surprised at how quiet it was. There were no cries from the people within, dodging the birds. Only crickets and the subtle slosh of waves in the distance. It would've been an otherwise pleasant night if only there wasn't a body hanging in the middle of the street.

He let out a quiet sob when he saw the corn cob bowl of the pipe jutting out of the dead man's mouth that could only belong to one person.

"Mr Dods! Who would do this to you?"

The old man's sideburns puffed out around the noose that had finished the job. The Mr Dods he knew wouldn't dare think of killing himself. That, coupled with the murder of his nephew and the unnatural behaviour of the ravens still inside with Tom and all of the pub's patrons, this couldn't have been a suicide. Though, if it were murder then wouldn't there be another box?

He exhaled, mustering enough courage to inspect the body. He stepped out into the street and noticed something quite odd. It was dark so he couldn't be sure, but he could've sworn the body was much too far from the building for the rope to be fastened to the second floor of the pub. It was as if the noose was suspended from the air itself.

Sufficiently satisfied that the box was nowhere upon the extremities of the body, he reached for Mr Dods's jacket. His fingers met the lump of something stuffed within the interior pocket.

He shook his head as the harsh lullaby repeated on end, crescendoing as his fingers neared the obstruction, anticipating another metal box full of teeth. It took all the courage he had to resist the urge to flee as he slipped his hand into the cloth. Barnaby drew in a sharp breath when his fingers grasped not a metal box, but a package wrapped in a slippery-like fabric. Pulling the package out, he removed it carefully from its silk encasement. Mr Dods's name was written in a bold scrawl across the top of the package, the corners of it torn where the dockmaster had opened it. He carefully reached within the opening, removing a folded piece of parchment within. How strange for so much packaging to be wrapped around a letter.

Unfolding it, he lifted the letter up towards the light of a nearby streetlamp to read it more clearly. There, in a bright red ink, an invitation was extended to Mr Dods to attend a private show at Mrs Dolly's Salon. It wasn't quite what Barnaby was expecting, yet not so out of the ordinary. What did alarm him was that not only did it personally address Mr Dods, it also featured a special guest appearance that caught his attention.

"Join us for an evening of allurement featuring Fraulein

Mystique, the dazzling slackwire and acrobatic contortionist extraordinaire of the *Beaumont Bros. Circus*."

Bile rose up in Barnaby's throat as he teetered on his heels, realizing he would have to call on his colleague after all. It was time Wilson Davies came out of retirement.

He then keeled over, his insides lurching onto Brunswick Street, more popularly known by the locals as Knock-'Em-Down Street.

2
WILSON'S RETIREMENT

The Detective's townhouse,
London, England

"Guard that station!" Wilson Davies's heart thumped loudly in his eardrums as he raced down the Port of London, desperately shouting at the incompetent Watchmen to secure the perimeter.

They were getting away. The butcher's daughter, who turned out to be a butcher of a different kind herself, and the dreadful circus freaks were bounding for the water's edge.

He was so close. Then a group of sailors knocked into him, pulling his attention from the circus for mere moments.

"Watch where you're going!" he growled, straightening his long black frock coat.

And just like that, the circus vanished into thin air. He spun around in a daze, scanning up and down the bustling port. They were nowhere to be seen. Replaying the whole scene in his head over, and over again, he knew he was missing something crucial. What was it? What had he failed to observe?

Wilson shot upright from his nightmare, his nightshirt

clinging to his chest and drenched in sweat. He took long, deep breaths to try and slow his skyrocketing heartbeat. Pulling back the covers, he swung his gangly legs over the edge of the bed and slipped his feet into silk slippers. He wouldn't be able to get back to sleep now, not with the images of losing the circus looping around in his mind on repeat. He clasped his hands tightly just thinking of it. He knew there was something so simple he'd overlooked. What could it be?

It was the only case he'd failed so spectacularly in solving and he didn't take the defeat lightly. Such pitfalls sent him into an obsessive trance so much so that he couldn't think clearly. It was worse than being without a case and drunk with boredom. In fact, that seemed preferable to this mess. Although calling the case at hand a 'mess' might be the most understated word to refer to the disarray of confusion he was experiencing as a result of taking on the *Beaumont Bros. Circus*.

Where was the order in all of this chaos? How could he lose not one, not two, but *five* people and two panthers so quickly? How had they outsmarted him so easily? Normally, he could spot what others could not and this gave him a great sense of pride. Yet, after that fateful day, he was reduced to obsessing over the events that lead him here over and over again.

Flaring his nostrils, he struck a match to light the lantern on his bedside table before making his way down the spiralling staircase to his favourite room in the three-story townhome he'd inherited from his aristocratic mother, God rest her. The library was nearly identical to the way she had it when he was a child, each shelf filled to the brim with leather-bound books she'd collected throughout her travels. There was hardly a book Wilson didn't have in his extensive library, although there were, on occasion, the rare opportunities that he was able to contribute to the collection by finding something new on economics or aeronautics. The only thing he insisted on changing were the couches arranged in the centre of the Persian rug. Wilson was determined to make the library his study and so his butler saw to it that most of his late mother's furniture be removed and replaced with a large, mahogany desk and armchair.

There, surrounded by endless literature, his work, and the warmth of the fireplace was the only place in his home where he could truly clear his mind. Which was precisely what he needed at that hour just before dawn. He needed to sweep the cobwebs this case had created in his mind and a gentleman was nothing if he didn't keep a tidy space from the inside out.

"Ooof!" He winced, stubbing his toe on the corner of the barley twist leg of his leather armchair. Heat rushed to his bruised foot and he set the lantern down with a loud clatter onto the top of his meticulously arranged desk. He didn't care who he woke. If he couldn't sleep, why should anyone else?

In the dim light of the shimmering lantern, he pulled the bronzed door handle of a cupboard within the desk. Without even bothering to look inside, he wrapped his hand around the neck of the bottle. To put the precious coca infused elixir even a few inches out of place would be unthinkable to him.

He retrieved a glass and, with a pop of the cork, tipped the bottle over the rim. When nothing but a deep burgundy droplet fell into the glass, Wilson tapped the bottom of the container. The hollowness of the bottle echoed louder with each attempt until Wilson hurled the useless thing at the fireplace, ricocheting against the marble encasement before shattering against the back of the firebox.

"HUBERT!" He bellowed, clenching and unclenching his shaky fists.

A thud followed by shuffling feet up the staircase from the basement met Wilson's ears and he tapped his foot impatiently.

"What is it, Mr Davies?" Hubert's monotonous voice replied, entering the library from the staircase hall.

The old man peered tiredly from behind his lit lamp, his rumpled tailcoat and trousers pulled over his nightshirt in haste.

"It seems as though my wine has been depleted."

Hubert furrowed his brows. "Shall I bring up a fresh bottle from the wine room, sir?"

"Not *that* wine." Wilson rolled his eyes. "The wine prescribed to me. Fetch me the doctor and tell him I'm experiencing mental fatigue so great it cannot possibly be satiated by a good night's rest."

"But, sir, at this hour—"

"Yes, at this hour," Wilson snapped, clasping his jittering fingers before gracefully closing the cupboard door. "I cannot focus on solving this case with all of the noise inside my head competing for my attention."

He paused, letting the deafening silence hang in the air. Hubert's unease was palpable, but Wilson's resolve was unquestionable.

"There's a murderer on the loose, Mr Hubert. I require the doctor."

"As you wish, sir." The old man's jowls quivered, lowering his head as he turned away to call on the doctor to bring his master's latest vice.

The clock on the marble mantle ticked endlessly, matching the drum of Wilson's fingers against the wood of his desk. His long leg draped over the other as he sat back in his chair, the other hand stroking the bristly beginnings of a beard he wasn't quite sure he liked when the echo of a door shutting and two faint voices in the distance alerted Wilson that the doctor had arrived.

Leaping from his chair, he dashed into the long hall bounding past the staircase to the entrance.

"Doctor Thorebourne, I'm most pleased to see you and I see you've won your losses back at the gentlemen's club—well done!" Wilson greeted the two startled men just as the doctor was pulling off his gloves.

"Yes, but how—?" The rather robust doctor's neck reddened, sharing a glance with the slightly older butler.

"Come, we've no time to waste." Wilson turned on his heel, marching back to the library.

The befuddled doctor ambled after the quick-footed Wilson down the narrow hall before suddenly stopping in front of the open door to his study. Wilson's tall, gangly frame towered beside the entrance, ushering the doctor inside. Dr Thorebourne promptly complied, making his way into the study surrounded by Wilson's vast library that had once impressed the doctor. It was now all too familiar to the doctor for him to spare even a glance about the room.

"Mr Davies." The doctor turned to face Wilson who remained at the threshold.

Wilson held up a finger and the doctor shut his mouth. "Mr Hubert, we shall require a pot of tea."

"Yes, sir," Hubert's tired voice echoed from down the hall.

"Doctor Thorebourne," Wilson began, finally stepping into the room, "I shall make this quick. I'm unable to focus, my head feels like there are a million bumbling bees within it and—"

"Mr Davies, I can't advise that you take any more of this tonic."

Wilson bit the side of cheek before clicking his tongue and taking a step back out into the hallway without turning around. "Mr Hubert!" He shouted. "That's a no to the tea."

He heard a faint mumble as Hubert acknowledged his withdrawal of the request and returned to the study, taking large strides to his armchair.

"Doctor Thorebourne, I don't think you understand the gravity of the situation."

The doctor took a deep breath, shaking his head. "I'm afraid I do, sir, and I can't condone it."

"Can't or won't?" Wilson lifted an impeccably groomed eyebrow.

"Won't." Dr Thorebourne lifted his chin.

"Your chemist says otherwise."

The doctor's mouth fell open. "How could you possibly know?"

"Never mind how I know there are other physicians in your practice willing to prescribe me whatever I want at a moment's notice." He inhaled audibly, trying to calm his temper. "We don't have to do all of that. *You* are my doctor and I'm feeling tired, now give me the tonic."

"The long-term effects still haven't been studied."

Wilson shrugged. "As you can see I'm in impeccable health."

Dr Thorebourne sighed, running a hand over his balding scalp. "Listen, Mr Davies, you're an incredibly gifted young man—"

"Thank you," Wilson interjected as the old doctor continued to ramble on, pacing back and forth across the rug.

The doctor stopped, waving his arm at Wilson. "I don't even know how you could possibly tell about my good fortune last night, but—"

"It's simple, really," Wilson interrupted once again, leaning back into his chair, "Despite the usual bags under your eyes from the recent late-night, your breath still smells of brandy mingled with the unmistakable cinnamon notes of your favourite celebratory cigar. A variety you rarely indulge in unless you have reason to commemorate such an occasion."

The doctor ceased his pacing to stare incredulously back at Wilson. He took it as a sign of triumph and continued. "That and you've still got your dinner jacket on."

Dr Thorebourne let out a brief chuckle, looking down as he fidgeted with the small envelope in his hands before making eye contact once again. "I believe you've just demonstrated for me quite the opposite of why you believe you need more of the tonic."

Wilson's nostrils flared, seething at the doctor who dared to take a step closer to his desk.

"I'm sorry. I can't in good conscience give you any more."

"Then why are you here?"

The doctor sighed. "I'm here as a friend."

Wilson smirked, lifting his skinny nose up into the air. "I don't think a friend would be so overjoyed to deliver such dreadful news that they'd come to see the results for themselves."

"I'm not—I wouldn't—" the doctor sputtered, his eyes bulging at the mere accusation. "Now listen here, Mr Davies, it's none of my business how you choose to squander your talents as long as you leave me and my practice out of it."

Wilson uncrossed his legs, standing to face the petite doctor at eye level.

"Now, I understand you are under a great deal of stress and so I suggest that you take some time off, leave somewhere for a while." Dr Thorebourne's lip quivered as he spoke, tossing the letter onto the desk between them. "This was on your doorstep. Perhaps it will give you some inspiration on where you should take your holiday."

With that, the doctor waved his goodbye before exiting, leaving Wilson Davies in the empty study just now dancing in the honey-gold luminescence of first light. Eyeing the envelope with suspicion, he finally picked it up and lowered back down into his armchair. His heartbeat nervously, remembering the last time a letter was left on his doorstep. He half expected it to be from the blasted Beaumont brothers themselves. He tossed the idea out of his mind after glancing at the postage stamp reading Nova Scotia. Hadn't his old friend mentioned this being his next destination?

Curiosity getting the better of him, he peeled the envelope open. He recognised Barnaby's signature calligraphy or lack thereof. Yet something was amiss. Wilson didn't even need to read the words to know that Barnaby was troubled when he wrote this letter. His frantic scrawl jetted out at odd times as if something or someone startled him sporadically throughout writing it.

"Dear Wilson," it began, *"I hate troubling... it is troubling, isn't it? I can't get it out of my head the..."* Wilson brought the letter inches from his face, studying the next few lines which were completely scratched out in black ink trying to decipher what his friend had decided not to tell him.

Clearly, his colleague wasn't in his right mind when he wrote this letter.

And what is that smell? He wondered, furrowing his brow as he took another whiff. It had a sweet aroma to it with a hint of something nutty. Sesame, perhaps? Hoping to shed some clues on the matter, Wilson scanned the rest of it.

"I can't get it out of my head, but I mustn't say what I must through the post. There are a great many forces at play here in Halifax, I daresay. Much like you've experienced before, only ten times over and nothing like it all at once..."

The letter went on in much the same nonsensical manner until the end when the long-winded Barnaby finally got to the point requesting—nay—*begging* Wilson to join him in Halifax to solve some mysterious case, the details of which his friend refused to share in the letter. It was almost as if the doctor had known he would be requested to leave town, but of course, that was impossible.

It wasn't until Wilson got to the last page that he noticed two things which stood out at him in an instant. The first was the smudge next to Barnaby's signature that was clearly not made by the ink he used to sign the letter, what with it being a bright shade of fuchsia. He scrunched his nose, sniffing the paper again. This time, instead of sweet nuts he got rose water, powdered sugar, and something of the citrus variety. He stuck his tongue out suddenly, licking the smudge.

"Lemon," he muttered to himself. "Precisely what I thought."

The second was in the postscript. *"The Beaumont Bros. Circus has struck again. Please, you must come at once..."*

3
THE BEAUMONT BROS. CIRCUS

*The outskirts of **Halifax***

The wheels of the carriage splashed along the winding road, the constant stream of raindrops dripping off the brim of Antoine's silk top hat before splattering against the floor of the driver's box. Sharp white bolts of lightning flashed across the inky sky before spiralling down towards the horseless drawn caravan. A young girl sat beside Antoine, her scarlet hair fluttering underneath the hood pulled over her as the swaying vehicle sped unnaturally towards the little peninsula on the outskirts of Halifax known as Deadman's Island.

The girl's hand shot out, catching the lightning that shot down from the sky within her palm. The energy zigzagged up and down her fingertips until she fluttered them, sending the electricity charging towards the wheels propelling them onward. The nearly invisible vehicle suddenly glowed as the energy pushed the wheels forward, driving along the Northwest Arm far from the boisterous nightlife of Brunswick Street and out of sight from the nosy neighbourhoods.

"Brava, Emma." Antoine looked down at the young girl beside him, a delighted gleam in his eye. "You're becoming quite the master of light manipulation."

"Thank you, sir." A sly grin spread across her face, her hazel eyes glowing yellow in the night, illuminating the path ahead.

A thump came from behind the large wood and metal trailer behind them followed by a ricochet of what could only be described as hundreds of marbles bouncing off the walls.

"Kizmet, stop!" Artus shouted over the storm from within the cabin.

A throaty growl shook the walls, a roar that could only belong to Absinthe defending her fellow panther. Antoine and Emma shared a knowing glance.

"It seems Absinthe and Kizmet are getting into trouble again." Emma chuckled.

Antoine shook his head, reaching back and pounding a fist against the compartment. The small window at the side opened and Artus stuck his head out into the pouring rain.

"How much longer can it be?" Artus's long, black hair was quickly drenched, clinging to his pale neck and angular cheekbones.

"We're nearly there, brother," Antoine assured, turning the steering wheel and guiding the caravan around the last bend.

Everyone was on edge, irritated from sleepless nights aboard the *Augustus* and the shipwreck they'd endured just a few hours before. Not to mention they weren't even supposed to be in Nova Scotia. When they discovered that they'd boarded the wrong ship it was too late. Despite all of this, Antoine reassured them his visions had shown him a new path and he was determined to make the most of the situation.

The road soon ended, bringing the caravan to a small forest surrounded by the gentle waves glittering in the moonlight. An owl hooted from somewhere above them in the darkened treetops. Across the Northwest Arm, the faint light of the town of Halifax could be seen in the distance, though not a single home or dock dared to be built on this forsaken peninsula.

"There, we should be safe here," Antoine said, offering Emma his arm and assisting her down from the driver's box.

The door of the caravan burst open just as two restless panthers leapt out, their giant paws landing soundlessly on the damp velvet grass as they went to investigate the little piece of land.

Artus hopped down from the compartment, followed by Timur and a reluctant Franziska, who stretched her hand out to ensure the rain had stopped before stepping out.

"Couldn't you have had a vision of us pitching camp a bit closer to town, brother?" Artus asked, whistling at Absinthe and Kizmet who were venturing off a little too far for comfort.

"Come now, Artus, where's your sense of adventure?" Antoine teased, arranging a few stray rocks into a fire ring. "Timur, would you go hunting for us? Perhaps take Absinthe and Kizmet with you."

Timur's eyes flashed red, illuminating his sorrel brown skin and curly, chin-length hair. With a quick nod, he disappeared in a blink of an eye.

"And make sure it's something that walks on all fours, this time," Artus muttered under his breath.

"Artus, would you fetch us some firewood?" Antoine asked his younger brother.

"Of course, dear brother." Artus bowed theatrically before scavenging through the darkened forest.

"Would you tell me about your vision that brought us

here?" Emma asked, picking up a rock and coming to stand next to Antoine. "Was the one to join us next on the *Augustus* with us? Were they the cause for that terrible crash?"

Antoine glanced up, taking the rock Emma offered and completing the ring. He brushed his hands together. "Well, my visions aren't so clear as all that. Particularly these days, I'm afraid."

"We shall have to go into town soon," Franziska said as she brought a small basket over from the caravan, her Prussian accent growing thicker in her tiredness. "Or we'll have to start seasoning our porridge with Artus's salty attitude."

She placed the basket next to the fire, winking at Emma who giggled just as Artus returned with the firewood.

"I heard that, Miss Franziska." Artus placed the pile in the centre of the fire ring Antoine had made.

"Oh, did you? Good," Franziska smirked, pulling out the few herbs and spices they had left from the basket.

"Emma," Antoine pointedly interrupted the banter between his brother and Franziska, waving a hand at the firewood. "Would you do the honours?"

"Of course," Emma said, taking a step back from the fire.

The rest of them followed suit, only taking a few more steps back just for good measure. Antoine had been training Emma to control her abilities. She was getting better, though there were a few times when she'd aim her power to light a lamp only to shatter the glass into dust.

Rubbing her hands together, she slowly peeled them apart slowly sending streaks of electricity as bright as the sun shooting between them. Sparks flew around her palms, the light reflecting in her eyes and illuminating her crimson hair. She flexed her fingers, methodically moving them until the energy formed a ball of lightning. Sparks shot out in every direction until she fluttered her fingers at the teepeed wood.

The wood erupted in flames instantly, sizzling and popping from the burning sap.

Franziska clapped her hands, coming to stand next to Emma. "Brava! I think you shall soon be ready for your first performance soon."

"You should tell that to Antoine." Emma smiled half-heartedly.

"Yes, why haven't we incorporated her light routine into our performances?" Artus folded his arms over his chest. "It's sure to be a crowd-pleaser."

Antoine stoked the fire, his brow wrinkling as he tried to hide his worry.

"You'd just need proper clothes," Franziska added, making a face at their drab brown disguises. "In fact, we all need to exchange our attire. I miss the trousers!"

The fire sparked as Antoine poked it one last time, tossing the stick aside before rising. "She's not ready."

"That's absurd, she's been training for months," Artus pointed out.

"I said, she's not ready," Antoine raised his voice and the three of them froze, staring at him with wide eyes.

A twig snapped behind them followed by the light tread of Kizmet and Absinthe returning from the forest, Timur followed them carrying the pheasant for their stew.

"Did I miss something?" Timur's deep voice cut through the tension in the air.

Emma looked at her hands, squeezing them together nervously. Antoine made no attempt at diffusing the situation, turning on his heel and retreating into the caravan. The ringleader had spoken, leaving the band of paranormal misfits in awkward silence.

"Nothing out of the ordinary," Franziska replied. "Excuse me."

"Be sure to talk some sense into that brother of mine,

won't you?" Artus called after her, grabbing the pheasant out of Timur's hands and taking a seat next to the fire to clean it.

Artus glanced up at Emma, whose eyes were squeezed tightly shut. He shook his head, focusing on the feathers he began plucking in handfuls. Kizmet let out a low grumble beside Artus, nudging his leg.

"Yes, go on. You don't need my permission to try and cheer her up," Artus replied, happy his panther had met another loyal friend.

After Emma had used her powers to magically heal Kizmet's nearly fatal gunshot wound, the panther took it upon himself to act as a guardian of sorts. Although, there wasn't much a panther could do to prevent Antoine from putting his foot in it.

Kizmet's loud, rumbling purr jolted Emma from her trance as he brushed against her and plopped beside her.

"Thank you, Kizmet." She rubbed behind his ears, sitting down beside him.

Emma looked over at Artus, who kept his eyes on the pheasant. Absinthe sat at his side, her protective eyes never leaving Kizmet. They were the cutest family Emma had ever witnessed, perhaps the only functional family, and she was proud to be part of it. Well, almost part of it, anyway.

She grimaced when she thought of Antoine's reaction whenever the subject of her performing with them came up. He was so supportive of her developing her powers, yet, for some reason, didn't want her to join them on stage. What had changed? Was it her? A tinge of fear pulled at her heart at the thought of Antoine reconsidering her being part of the circus. What if they left her behind? She had nowhere else to go.

While Emma contemplated her position among them, Franziska was trying to get to the bottom of Antoine's aversion to her joining them.

"What was that all about?" The caravan door closed behind her with a click.

Antoine stood with his back to her, about to climb the ladder to their makeshift room in the loft. He glanced over his shoulder, sighing. "She's not ready."

"That's not true and you know it." Franziska crossed her arms, tapping her foot impatiently. "She's excelling in all of Timur's juggling lessons and in my sessions, she is on her way to being a much better wheel gymnast than I'll ever be. Not to mention she's constantly practising to control her light manipulation power!"

"It's not about her talent. She's become a wonderful performer."

Franziska took a step forward, waving her arms. "Then let her perform."

He slowly turned to face Franziska, unable to look her in the eye as he fidgeted with a stray thread of the rope strapping the floor of their stage up so that it doubled as one of the walls of the caravan.

Franziska furrowed her glittery eyebrows. "You've seen something, haven't you?"

"Yes." He ran a hand over his neatly combed black hair, parted at the side and trimmed short.

"Please." Franziska removed the little bit of space between them, coming to rest her hands on his shoulders. "Tell me what troubles you."

Antoine stole a few breaths before replying, wrapping his hands around hers. "It's more of a feeling. Whenever the subject of her performing with us comes up there's… there's this music that plays in my ear. It's like a… a tin flute. The wretched sound fills me with a darkness I can't even describe. It's this sense that something's coming for her."

His smoky eyes turned to charcoal. "It's coming for us all."

4
THE PECULIAR CASE OF BARNABY GREY

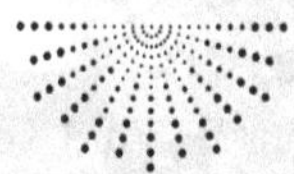

A busy dock along Upper Water St

Wilson Davies swung his black frock coat on over his matching vest and trousers, quickly disembarking the ship after it was sufficiently moored to one of the wharves along the Halifax Harbour, several of which he'd noticed had sustained considerable damage.

"You there, good sir," Wilson greeted a stout man with a ledger. He assumed by the ledger the old man held that he must've been the dockmaster and so he made his way to the greying man.

Wilson tipped his top hat in greeting, sizing the man up and observing by the way others interacted with him that if someone were to know anyone in this port it would be him. "Might I trouble you for a moment? I've just arrived and am looking for a man. He goes by Barnab—"

"Barnaby Grey, yeah I know 'em," the gruff man said, puffing a pipe with a corncob bowl jutting out of his mouth. "What's it to ye?"

"I'm an old friend of Barnaby's and he sent me a letter demanding that I visit and, well, I had to oblige, you see."

The greying man eyed him suspiciously through the billowing smoke. "Then let me see it."

"See it?" Wilson lifted a brow, leaning forward to ensure he heard the old man right.

"The letter." The man stretched his pudgy free hand out. "Barnaby's been through a lot and don't need anyone both-erin' him so le' me see this letter."

"Well, all right," Wilson said, clicking his tongue in distaste. He hadn't given this man any reason to distrust him but complied with the dockmaster out of delighted anticipa-tion of showing the older man he was wrong. "I really don't see what all the fuss is about. It's all in there."

The man snatched the letter from Wilson, glancing through the first few lines of it. He took particular care in analysing the signature.

"And what's this?" The man asked, pointing to the pink smudge.

"Ah." Wilson lowered his gaze, trying to pull a smile from his face and remain serious. "I admit I was partaking in a good deal of port when I received this letter, you understand. Now, if everything's in order, won't you please tell me where Barnaby resides?"

The man stroked his grey sideburns thoughtfully, finally handing the letter back to Wilson Davies with a sigh. "It does appear to be from Barnaby."

"As I said, I'm an old friend." Wilson lifted his chin high, tucking the correspondence back into a pocket within his frock coat. "And you are?"

"Mr Dods," the dockmaster replied, tucking the ledger under his left arm and stretching his other out.

"Detective Wilson Davies, a pleasure to meet your acquaintance." Wilson shook the old man's hand firmly.

"Ye share the same trade as Detective Grey, I see. Well, ye'll have to forgive me, Detective Davies." Mr Dods sniffed, wiping his nose. "Ye can't be too careful, especially now after what Detective Grey's lost. He doesn't need no trouble."

"Lost?" Wilson arched a brow.

"Ye haven't heard?" Mr Dods shook his head, looking to be on the verge of tears making Wilson shift uncomfortably. "Detective Grey lost his nephew not two weeks ago. Been boarded up in his flat ever since."

Wilson gave an understanding nod. "Seems like I've come not a moment too soon."

With that, Mr Dods motioned for Wilson to follow him before hollering to a young dock labourer as he walked by.

"John, get this man here's luggage," Mr Dods ordered, gruffly. "We're takin' 'em to George street and Grafton."

"Yes, sir," the young lad named John replied, smushing his cloth cap over his dishevelled hair and briefly making eye contact with Wilson before rushing down the dock to fetch the luggage.

Wilson froze, the pale scar below the young lad's left eye triggering a feeling of recognition. He'd seen this scar from somewhere before. However, that was absurd. Wilson had never been to Halifax before now. Shaking the feeling of déjà vu, he pressed on, keeping stride with Mr Dods as the dock labourer followed behind.

The dock groaned under the stomping boots of the many seamen and dockers making their way to and from the port town that stretched out along the entire coastline beyond the waterfront.

"Would you mind if I ask how Barnaby's nephew died?" Wilson asked, having to raise his voice above the rowdy fish market they passed. "I thought his nephew resided somewhere in Scotland with his sister."

"He was coming to visit the poor detective. Had high

hopes for the visit, too. Detective Grey planned on training 'em to be a detective."

"Sounds just like the old boy." Wilson chuckled.

"Then the storm came blowin' through the harbour, ye see, completely demolishin' many of the docks along Lower Water. Even caused the Gas Works plant to explode!"

Wilson nodded. "I noticed that when I arrived."

"Never seen anythin' like it my whole life, and I've seen my fair share of storms rollin' through here. Halifax is not for the faint of heart."

"I've no doubt of that," Wilson replied as they made their way through a small park across from a frame building with a steeple and a sign reading *St Paul's Episcopal Church*. "And what about it was so out of the ordinary?"

Mr Dods harrumphed, turning to him as they stopped in front of a soap factory on the corner. "Well, for starters when the *Augustus* towing the young lad came into the harbour, the water rose up like a giant tornado, like none I've ever seen before. Then the waters turned from blue to a shade pinker than Mrs Dolly's lips before turning blood red."

Wilson listened as he scanned the endless rooftops along George street until he spotted a break in the buildings where the street ended. "Mrs Dolly, you say? And who's that?"

"Er..." Mr Dods's face flushed crimson, turning his back on Wilson as he continued to lead them down a few more blocks. "Just a fine woman of an establishment off of Brunswick Street. Nobody important to the storm or the death of Detective Grey's nephew, mind ye."

"Of course," Wilson said, taking note of the old man's uncomfortableness at the subject and shelving it for future reference if needed.

Mr Dods quickly changed the subject, pointing out various buildings of importance that they passed by. As they neared the end of George Street, Wilson eyed a spectacular whitewashed clock tower and, behind it, a great fortress atop a hill vacant of any other buildings protruding out behind the rest lining the street.

"And what's that building there?" Wilson asked, pointing to it.

Mr Dods followed Wilson's gaze to the stone building perched above the rest. "Ah, that's the Citadel. Ye'll never see a more capable defence than she."

"I see." Wilson eyed the vantage point, noting that it would have the perfect, unobstructed view of the Gas Works plant and the harbour beyond it. Anyone manning the tower would've seen the other-worldly storm Mr Dods described.

"Well, this is where we part," Mr Dods said, halting in front of a three-storey brick house with a truncated roof with a single attic window. "Detective Grey lives in the top flat."

"Thank you so much for all of your help." Wilson tipped his top hat once more.

"Take care of Detective Grey, and be careful, will ye? Strange things are brewing," Mr Dods replied with a gruff farewell before instructing John to see that Wilson's bags were brought up.

It wasn't long before Wilson made it up the short flight of stairs to the street door, the dead flower stems left unpruned for the winter in the window boxes along the first floor left him anticipating the lack of cleanliness within.

Swinging the simple cast iron door knocker, he rapped it several times. A moment later, an elderly woman with wisps of grey hair flying from her sloppy updo opened the door.

"Yes?" Her shaky voice asked, narrowing her eyes at Wilson and the young lad carrying his suitcases. "We've no vacancies."

"Yes, of course, madam." Wilson removed his hat, giving a small bow. "But I'm not here to rent a flat. I'm here to see Mr Barnaby Grey. The detective. Does he reside here?"

She sized up the elaborately dressed detective before her who was arguably more fit for a dinner party than calling on an old friend.

"Follow me." Without another word, she turned on her heel and hobbled down the dimly lit corridor.

"Come on," Wilson said to the young lad, unable to meet his eye without having the painfully annoying sensation that they'd met somewhere before.

They'd barely stepped foot in the musty foyer the width of two full-grown men standing shoulder to shoulder when the woman came to a halt. She turned back at them, hunched over a gleaming birchwood finished walking cane. It was probably the cleanest thing in this place, Wilson mused, and, by the height of it being disproportional to the woman, assumed it to be an heirloom from a much taller relative. She rapped the bottom of her cane on the wooden bannister at the corner, hidden by a bit of wallpaper peeling from the wall.

"It's the only door on the top floor," she said in a monotonous tone.

Wilson grimaced. "I'm much obliged."

"And tell him he's late on rent." The woman called over her shoulder, grumbling something else under her breath before disappearing in one of the many cobwebbed doors.

The staircase groaned under Wilson's light tread, making him fear he'd fall right through. The mere thought of what foul rodents might be waiting for him deep below made him lightheaded. He'd never imagined the Barnaby Grey who trained alongside him in the art of deduction taking up occupancy at such an establishment. Although, Barnaby did have a tendency to be exorbitantly more curious in the exotic than he. That was one of the main reasons they parted ways when Barnaby received a case that took him to Istanbul while Wilson remained in London. In fact, Wilson hadn't been so far from home in quite some time.

Whatever will Hubert do with all of his free time? Wilson wondered.

Reaching the top of the stairs, Wilson knocked on the door preparing to greet his oldest and, quite possibly, only friend.

"Just leave those there." Wilson bid the young dock labourer farewell, giving him a few coins for his trouble before he disappeared back down the dreary stairwell.

"Ah," Wilson sighed, happy to finally be at his destination.

Turning back to the room door, Wilson frowned when it remained shut. He'd expected Barnaby to have answered by now. Perhaps he didn't hear the knock?

Straightening his solid black vest, he rapped three more times and brought his ear to the door.

A loud kerplunk followed by shuffling feet met his ear. To his great horror, the decibel of the feet combined with the ricochet of something metal told him he'd probably awoken a rat. Wilson squeezed his eyes shut.

"Barnaby!" He rapped on the room door several more times. This time loud enough that his friend was sure to have heard him.

A kerfuffle of indiscernible words from one of the back rooms met Wilson's ears before the door finally swung open.

"You're here!" Barnaby greeted him, still in his nightshirt even though it was well into the evening. "But are you really here?"

Wilson narrowed his eyes. "Why, of course, I'm here, Barnaby. Whatever would I be if I wasn't?"

Barnaby's eyes widened, frantically waving him inside. Wilson picked up his suitcases and marched in, glancing over his shoulder at his old friend who clung to the doorframe, jerking his head from left to right like he was expecting someone else to follow him inside.

"I just met your landlady," Wilson commented, "Quite friendly."

His old friend let out a high pitched yelp before closing the door, breathless as if he'd just run up a flight of stairs.

"You've met Mrs Mable, have you now?" Barnaby shook his head. "She'll be wanting her rent, though I can't for the life of me remember where I've put it."

"I'm sure I could help with that," Wilson replied.

Barnaby remained with his back glued to the door and Wilson raised a brow. "Are you all right?"

It took Barnaby several moments before he could peel himself away from it.

"Yes, yes, fine." He stepped over a pile of old dishes placed upon platters that seemed as though they'd been waiting to be removed for some time. Barnaby scratched the back of his head. "Sorry for the mess. Please, have a seat."

Barnaby turned to the only chair in the whole flat which had a wall of dusty books and old newspaper clippings piled upon it. "Ha!" He let out an astonished laugh as if he were surprised to see the stack. "Let me clear this for you."

Grabbing the books, he carefully placed them next to the overstuffed built-in bookcases framing the only window in the little flat.

Wilson opened his mouth to question Barnaby about the mess, but remembered he'd just lost his nephew and figured now was not the time. Instead, he smiled appreciatively and took a seat.

"Thank you," he said, removing his top hat and placing it on his knee. "I received your letter."

"Hmm? My letter?" Barnaby pushed a pile of old laundry off of a footstool placed in front of what looked to be a miniature piano cluttered with little frames and boxes dispersed between hardened wax melting over short candlesticks. "Oh, yes the letter! I'm so glad you're here, Wilson. We will sort all of this out now that you're here."

Barnaby suddenly leapt up from his perch, eyes wide as they glazed over, staring off into space. "Do you hear it?"

"Hear what?" Wilson asked, turning in his seat to see what Barnaby could possibly be looking at, yet nothing was there.

"The music." Barnaby shuddered, shutting his eyes momentarily before diving back down to the footstool, sliding the cover of the piano to reveal the ivory keys.

Wilson's nostrils flared as he tried to curb his growing impatience, removing the letter from his coat pocket. "Barnaby, I beg of you to—"

The man spiralling into madness interrupted him by hitting the keys one at a time and humming a horridly off-pitch tune so dreadful Wilson couldn't possibly fathom it being a real song.

"Barnaby Grey," Wilson snapped, finally raising his voice, startling the frazzled man much too large for the little footstool he sat on. "I know this must be a hard time for you and I can't imagine what you must be going through, what with losing your nephew and all, but I'm here to help."

"Archie…" Barnaby moaned, grasping his shaking hands and glancing out the window.

Wilson leaned forward, carefully watching his friend. "What happened exactly?"

Barnaby licked his lips, blinking rapidly a few times before meeting Wilson's gaze. "I-I was at Fairbanks Wharf where the *Augustus* was planned to dock. I was speaking with Mr Dods about the peculiar ducks… boxes of teeth…" His lip trembled. "Oh no, not Mr Dods, too! I heard the music and knew, I-I just *knew* something horrible had happened. I never would have thought it would be to poor Mr Dods!"

"What exactly happened to Mr Dods?" Wilson drew his eyebrows together. Mr Dods hadn't mentioned anything horrible happening to *himself,* but perhaps it wasn't his business or pertinent to the case?

"He's *dead*!"

Wilson let out a sudden bark of laughter, startling his friend.

"You would *laugh* at such news?" Barnaby stood up, shaking his head as he began to pace. "Your morbid sense of humour astounds me, Wilson."

"This must be some kind of a joke." Wilson wiped the moisture from his eyes. "Unless you're not talking about Mr Dods the dockmaster and there's some other man who goes by the same name."

Barnaby froze in his tracks. "You knew Mr Dods?"

"*Knew* him? No. I met him when I arrived earlier today. He's the one who escorted me here."

"That's not possible." Barnaby stepped over the assorted piles blocking the curtained door frame to an adjoining room. "I promise you I saw him hanging by a noose outside of the Two Crows. I heard the music. It's why I sent you that letter. I can prove it. Just wait."

"What's this all about?" Wilson called after Barnaby who disappeared behind the curtain. "About hearing some sort of music?"

"Here," Barnaby said, rushing back into the room, knocking over one of the many towers cluttering the floor. He didn't pay the obstacles any attention.

Wilson eyed the folded piece of parchment with suspicion, not wanting to engage in Barnaby's delusions. With a sigh, he finally caved, taking it from his friend. It was an advertisement for a performance the *Beaumont Bros. Circus* would be performing. He chuckled to himself, thinking how foolish this circus was going to look when he showed up to arrest them once and for all. He glanced at the date, noticing it was in a few days. He'd be sure to be there.

Eyeing the location, he smirked. "Ah, now I see why Mr Dods seemed reluctant to say which establishment Mrs Dolly runs. However, I fail to see how this notice proves that he's dead."

"Because I took it from his dead body."

Wilson's mouth fell open at this proclamation. Either his friend was prophetic and had a vision of the dockmaster dying or he was entirely mad. Wilson refused to even consider the former but dreaded the latter more than anything.

Without warning, Barnaby flung a sack coat over his nightshirt and bounded for the room door.

"Where are you going?" Wilson called after Barnaby just as he swung the door open.

Barnaby turned back. "If Mr Dods is alive as you say he is, I must see for myself."

"You don't even have proper clothing on!" Wilson protested a bit too late as Barnaby had already descended the first flight of stairs and was well out of earshot. "What have I gotten myself into?"

Against his better judgment, he followed Barnaby out of the decrepit building. Wilson's long stride easily caught up with his friend's rather short frame sprinting down towards Upper Water Street. After passing the busy market where they were greeted with looks of disapproval followed by whispers of Barnaby's indecency, they came to a halt at the edge of E Morrison's Wharf where Wilson had first met Mr Dods.

"My eyes must be deceiving me," Barnaby gasped in disbelief.

There, at the end of the dock, yelling at the dock labourers was none other than the heavyset dockmaster.

"Is he the one you saw dead?" Wilson watched his friend carefully.

"Yes." Barnaby scratched his head. "How is he alive?"

He noted that Barnaby's eyes never wavered, there was no indication that he doubted the man he saw now was the same man he'd witnessed outside of the Two Crows. He didn't look away or fidget unnecessarily, all signs of deception. His friend was telling the truth, or at least what Barnaby had been led to believe was the truth. Wilson was beginning to believe it was no coincidence that the *Beaumont Bros. Circus* was in town at the same time as Archie's death and Barnaby's growing hysteria. He wasn't sure what the connection was, but he was certain this time he would catch the criminal behind this. They would pay for the trauma they were causing his friend.

Wilson placed his hand on Barnaby's shoulder, meeting his eye. "I swear to you, I shall not rest until I find out what's going on here."

Barnaby glanced heavenward, a sigh of relief escaping him. "Thank you for believing me."

Wilson bit his cheek, unsure he quite believed everything his friend told him, yet refrained from divulging this since it wasn't pertinent. "I will need you to walk me through everything you've been through. Any detail you can remember. We shall leave no rock unturned." He spun Barnaby to face the direction they came from. "However, first, you must get some rest. There's no hope of us solving anything with you in this state."

His friend made no objections, allowing Wilson to guide him back down George street. Though Wilson appeared optimistic, there was a question tugging at his confidence that filled him with dread. It was as ominous as the hooded hangman cleaning the gallows they passed. Was there even a case to be solved here? Or was all of this just the delusions of an unwell man?

5
A WELL MAN

BARNABY WASN'T sure if it was just a dream, or if he really did hear a screeching noise. It was only after an alarming clatter from the front room that he snapped upright, his nightcap falling to the floor.

"Wilson, is that you?" He massaged his arm that had fallen asleep, every joint in his body aching as he manoeuvred himself to sit at the edge of his bed.

Rubbing the sleep from his eyes, he reached for his cigarette case he kept on a pile of books beside his bed, but his fingers returned empty. His eyes flew open and gasped.

All of his stacks he'd arranged about the room were gone. In their stead were a lint covered rug and various pieces of furniture he never remembered being there. "WILSON!"

"Yes, Barnaby?" Wilson stuck his head through the embroidered curtain he barely recognised.

"Where's my cigarette case?"

"It's on the dresser there"—Wilson pointed to a solid oak bedroom dresser with multiple drawers and an oval mirror on the body of it. Beside it, a suit he hadn't donned in quite some time hung pressed for him—"I've also taken the liberty of doing some minor housekeeping. If we've got a case to solve, I must have a tidy space. You know what I always say. The two most important things of a respectable man…."

Wilson disappeared behind the curtain again.

"Cleanliness and order, yes I know." Barnaby grimaced. If he was being honest with himself he didn't feel very respectable. "And where did you get the furniture?"

"I went to Talmage & Sons on the corner of Prince and Barrington upon Mrs Mable's recommendation!" Wilson called through the curtain, before popping back in. "Dear Barnaby, please do put on proper clothes. I could use your help. I can't for the life of me figure out where these go."

"No! Don't touch that!" Barnaby flew from his bedside, snatching the metal box from Wilson's grasp.

"What are they? You've hundreds of them scattered about."

"They're not scattered." Barnaby snapped, brushing past Wilson and scanning the front room for the rest of them. "I had everything organized by location. Each box. Where did you put the boxes from the tub?"

Wilson blinked, giving a rather confused look. "I put them on the table over there so that the tub could be used. Please tell me you still *bathe*."

Barnaby ignored Wilson's question, rushing over to the larger of the four small groups of identical boxes. He picked one from the top, gingerly holding it between his thumb and index finger and holding it up into the light cascading from the window. It was much too bright in Barnaby's mind, but Wilson had a process and he was his only hope if they were going to figure out who killed his nephew.

"In each of these boxes contains a pouch of teeth," Barnaby began, turning to face his friend. "Each box was found on the victims of horrific and rather confusing crimes."

"Intriguing." Wilson stroked the stubble on his chin, taking a seat at the now immaculate table placed by the window. "Please, do tell me more. And don't spare any last detail."

Barnaby took a seat opposite Wilson, arching a brow when Wilson made no attempt to retrieve a notebook or a fountain pen.

"Aren't you going to write this down?"

Wilson frowned. "Whatever for?"

"To keep track of your notes, of course!"

"Don't be silly, you know I don't need one." Wilson chuckled. "Besides, the safest place for notes is for them to remain locked up here." Wilson tapped his temple. "Now, tell me what happened."

Barnaby huffed, placing the box next to his collection, tracing the pyramids engraved on the top lid with his finger. "It all began with the ducks…"

Beaumont Bros. Circus,
Visiting the market on Upper Water St

Emma smiled, breathing in the crisp morning breeze so delighted to be out of the campsite. She didn't know what it was about the forest that surrounded them, but she always felt a presence watching her. It bothered her so much so that sleep proved difficult.

Yet now, out in the fresh air, she could've skipped down the bustling street next to Franziska and Timur without a care in the world. If only Antoine hadn't warned them they needed to keep a low profile and not do anything to draw attention to themselves while they were in town. Which was why Artus was left to watch over the camp and his panthers. The thought of marching down the busiest street in Halifax flanked by Absinthe and Kizmet made Emma giggle.

"We should split up to make the most of this, but *please* be careful, all right?" Antoine said, coming to a halt on the corner of the city market. "We've no idea how this city will react to us."

"Don't worry." Franziska grinned, placing an arm over Emma's shoulder as she tucked her other hand inside the pocket of her trousers she'd made from the muddy-brown dress Antoine had given her. "We'll blend right in."

Antoine sighed, shaking his head in disapproval and Emma's laughter deepened. If it wasn't Franziska's trousers that destroyed their cover of normalcy, it'd be her snowy white hair pinned in curls on top of her head. She'd refused to cover it per Antoine's suggestion by reminding him that she loved him, but would never take fashion advice from him.

"All right, you take Emma and buy what we need from the market." Antoine motioned for Timur. "Timur and I will split up to find the perfect spot to perform."

With that, Antoine and Timur bid their farewell and went off in opposite directions. Emma followed Franziska, who perused the many wooden crates of the vendors strewn along the street, the sounds of bartering and the clop of horses' hooves echoing around them.

Her stomach grumbled when the waft of the yeast in fresh bread met her nostrils. It'd been so long since she'd smelled anything so delicious it made her mouth water.

"Franziska, may I go explore for a few moments?" She asked Franziska who was examining a cabbage, unable to take any more of the temptation of the market and wanting to see more of the port city.

"When was this picked?" Franziska asked the stout vendor eyeing them suspiciously.

"All of the cabbages are the freshest this side of the Northwest Arm," the man replied with a huff.

Franziska gave a tight smile, paying before placing the cabbages in her basket. She glanced down at the expectant Emma, pressing her lips together. "Antoine instructed us to stay together. We won't be here long."

"Oh, please!" Emma folded her hands together, batting her long eyelashes.

Franziska sighed. "Fine, but meet me at that corner here within the hour. And be *careful.*"

She nodded before escaping the crowded market and following the sound of the waves crashing against the timbers of the docks lining Upper Water street as far as the eye could see. Taking a deep breath she revelled in the little bit of freedom, taking it all in. The smell of raw fish from the market mingled with the crisp salt sweeping in the breeze from the harbour. Seamen shouted, their raised voices disappearing in the wailing foghorn of an incoming ship. It all took her breath away, her fair cheeks flushing in happiness that seemed endless now since she'd left London. No more did she have to cower from the monsters she was raised by, or of being taken away from the *Beaumont Bros. Circus*. She was, for the most part, one of them and one day she prayed to have the opportunity to perform alongside them as a true circus member. It was quite fun only having to camouflage her power on the guise of her routine. It was like hiding in plain sight, and the thrill of it sent her heart racing in the best way possible.

"Watch it," an old man said gruffly when she nearly ploughed right into him, so deep in thought, she forgot to look where she was going.

"So sorry," she said, watching the stout man rushing down the sidewalk. She frowned. "Mr Dods?"

The man froze, forcing other pedestrians to sidestep to avoid crashing into him as well. He turned slowly, his greying hair and bristly sideburns sticking out at all angles. Emma smiled, happy to see a familiar face. After the *Augustus* crashed through the Halifax Harbour, dockmaster had been the one who'd helped her and the rest of the circus get situated. He'd even shown them the way to one of the many carriage factories where they'd gotten their caravan. Of course, they had to make a few adjustments themselves to make it the home it was to them now, Mr Dods had been a great help to them.

"I thought that was you." She marched up to him, smiling brightly. "Do you remember? It's me, Emma. You pulled me and the rest of my... er, family out after the shipwreck a few weeks ago."

Mr Dods cleared his throat, his eyes darting around. "Y-yes, of course. How are you fairing?"

"Quite well, thank you. I was wondering," she began, glancing down at the man's hands that couldn't seem to keep still.

The dockmaster fidgeted with something small and square in his hands, quickly pocketing it when Emma's gaze was drawn to it. "Yes, what is it? I'm in quite a hurry."

"Of course, I won't keep you much longer," Emma replied. "I was just wondering if you happened to know of anyone in town looking for entertainers? A circus to be exact."

"A circus? None that I can think." Mr Dods glanced about, pulling his bowler hat from his head and wiped the sweat from his forehead on his sleeve. "Although ye'r older sister might find some luck at Mrs Dolly's. They're always looking for guest entertainment. Tell 'em I sent ye. Best be off now."

The man scuttled off across the street, nearly getting run

over by a wagon passing by. Emma frowned, wondering why Mr Dods was in such a hurry. Of course, she didn't know the man and so she decided not to waste her last few minutes of exploration worrying needlessly. She skipped past a city well as a woman struggled to pull the tangled windlass, ducked around a docker carting a load of crates from a nearby ship, and raced to the end of the dock without a care in the world. She just wanted to be closer to the sea.

Gazing fondly as the wind caused the glass waters to ripple, the reflection of the sun casting a glow of energy across its surface only she could see and appreciate. She remembered how terrified she was before sneaking onto the ship with Franziska and the circus, never travelling on a boat before, but that was before experiencing the magical rush of being surrounded by the ocean's energy. There was nothing like it and now she wished she could do it all over again.

She smirked, knowing Antoine probably mirrored her sentiment except for a much different reason. Little did any of them know that when they snuck into the fish bins to escape being caught by the detective that they'd snuck onto the *Augustus* instead of their intended ship headed for America.

Glancing over her shoulder to ensure no one would see her, she stretched her hands out towards the water, spreading her fingers wide and gracefully fluttering her fingers to the beat of the waves. The light on the water directly in front of her popped and sparked until beads of seawater floated like diamonds, rising up to dance under her palm. She snapped her fingers again and the dancing diamonds popped like bubbles sending the energy raining back down into the ocean.

A sudden gust of wind whipped her crimson locks about her face and neck and she revelled in it, closing her eyes and enjoying the methodical lullaby of the wind lapping its way through the harbour.

Emma's eyes flew open when a woman wailed from the city well behind her, sending a flock of startled doves into the air. She turned, shading her eyes from the sun and quickly followed the rush of people running to see what happened. A crowd quickly formed around the city well making it difficult to see. Carefully ducking around a group of women, one of which teetered on her heels on the verge of fainting. When Emma stepped around them, her heart plummeted, spotting what all the commotion was about.

There, tangled in the rope, a human arm dangled above the bucket of water being drawn. That wasn't the only thing that made Emma's heart race. It was the sapphire shoes of the well-dressed man all in black with a long frock coat leaning so far over the side of the well his head disappeared. She would recognise those lace-up sapphire boots anywhere.

"Barnaby, come look at this," the man's voice echoed from the well, calling to his much shorter colleague who fidgeted with the collar of his sack coat, standing as far from the severed arm as he could.

The man with the sapphire shoes straightened, pulling his head out of the well. "There's more down there. A great deal more."

Emma licked her lips, unable to move. She was within just a few feet of Detective Wilson Davies, the one who'd been so close to arresting her for murder. What would happen if he saw her now? Would he recognise her? Not wanting to take any chances, she pulled the hood of her cloak over to cover her hair.

A whistle blew and a group of armed officers ran towards the peculiar duo, shoving past her, and gaining the detective's attention. Emma's breath caught in her throat, suppressing a cry as she quickly lowered her gaze. She had to get out of there before he spotted her if it wasn't too late already.

"Excuse me," her voice shook, trying to get through the crowded sidewalk and back to the market. Franziska was probably worried sick.

Her muscles tightened preparing to run, the sensation of being watched sending the hairs on the back of her neck standing upright. She glanced over her shoulder, regretting it the moment she spotted the detective in the distance looking in her direction. Holding her breath, she forced her stiff legs into a sprint across Upper Water street praying to God the detective didn't recognise her.

6
THE CLOSE ENCOUNTER

THE DETECTIVE IGNORED the raucous from the officers shouting at him for some answers about what happened, so focused on the crowd surrounding them. There'd been someone there, someone with a wisp of red hair he recognised. But where did she go? And was it really her? Or was he imagining things?

Before he could run into the crowd searching for her, the severed arm he'd forgotten he was holding was snatched from his hands by an officer, pulling his wrists behind his back and handcuffing him.

"What's the meaning of this?" Wilson cried. "Barnaby, please tell these men who we are."

"I'm trying to," Barnaby replied, glancing back at Wilson. All the colour drained from his face when he spotted the mangled arm, greying with splotches of cuts and scrapes from where it detached from its body. "Listen, this is Wilson Davies, my colleague. I can guarantee that he had no involvement with this crime and if you let us work we'll be able to find you the true culprit."

The officer narrowed his eyes at Wilson who frowned in response. "Who's to say we haven't found him already."

"Ha!" Wilson let out a short laugh.

Barnaby sent him a look of warning before turning back to the officer. "Because this is *Detective* Wilson Davies. He works with me."

The officers shared a glance at one another before finally unlocking the handcuffs with a click. "He's in your custody now, Detective Grey."

"Thank you," Barnaby sighed, his shoulders relaxing. "Thank you so much."

"You must be quite blind, dear officer," Wilson said, rubbing his wrists.

"Wilson!" Barnaby gasped.

"What? It's true." Wilson shrugged. "Just look at the pink blisters about the arm. And the swelling. Did you *see* the swelling? The body looks more like a whale with prunes for fingers. I would guess this body has been in the well for one… maybe two days?"

The officer who handcuffed him sneered. "Now listen here, *Detective*—"

"And I would bet"—Wilson dashed for the well—"I'll find more proof of this once you pull the rest of this man out."

"Th-there's more?" Barnaby stuttered, swallowing obviously.

"Why, of course," Wilson replied. "An arm is usually accompanied by the rest of its body."

"I think I'm going to be sick." The shorter man fanned himself with a violet handkerchief, leaning against the stone surrounding the well for support but then quickly stepped away from it when the officers started fishing the dead body from it.

Wilson frowned. "You've changed, Barnaby. I remember you showing off like your stomach was made of steel, taking on the most gruesome of cases during our years of training. What happened?"

"That was all for show." Barnaby dabbed his forehead with the bright cloth, tucking it back into the pocket of his matching waistcoat before securing the buttons of his sack coat. "I wanted to impress, although I was never without a bucket or a bag just in case. I'm not so young and foolish anymore."

"I see." Wilson pondered this for a moment before changing the subject. "Where shall the autopsy be performed, then?"

Barnaby cringed. "I believe Doctor Larson over on Bishop Street is in charge of such things."

Wilson turned to the officers. "When the body had been delivered to Doctor Larson, send a message to the residence of Barnaby Grey—"

Barnaby cleared his throat, gaining Wilson's attention and shaking his head.

"No?" Wilson raised an eyebrow, studying the shorter man as he checked his pocket watch. "Ah, yes you're quite right, Barnaby. What was I thinking? Make that the Halifax Club on Hollis Street, good sirs."

Wilson straightened his top hat, not waiting for a response from the officers before motioning for Barnaby to follow him. "I can see we're both in need of a drink."

Barnaby chuckled to himself, grasping his shaking hands and quickening his steps to meet Wilson's long stride.

"I'm glad to see you haven't lost your gift," Barnaby said.

"Nonsense, Barnaby," Wilson said, leading the way across Upper Water Street. "Deduction is not a gift, it's an art. Dear me, have you forgotten our training so quickly?"

"I must admit I was never as good at it as you..." Barnaby trailed, his eyes suddenly darting down a darkened street. He could've sworn he saw that foreign docker, yet when he blinked the man was gone.

Wilson furrowed his brows, wondering what his friend was staring at, although he didn't have the patience to ask and left it at that. Passing the market in silence, the two had no idea that the members of the *Beaumont Bros. Circus* were merely an arm's reach away.

"EMMA!" Franziska cried, pulling her into a hug when she reached the market. "Where've you been? I've been worried sick. Antoine went to search for you!"

"I'm sorry," Emma replied, unable to make contact as her stomach was still doing somersaults from nearly being seen by the detective. "I was just at the end of one of the docks and then—"

"There you are," Antoine's interrupted, walking up the sidewalk to join them. "How could you leave when I *explicitly* told you to stay with Franziska?"

"I—" Emma tried to explain.

"Antoine, it was me. She wanted to go exploring and so I gave her permission," Franziska said.

Antoine rubbed his neck in frustration, turning around to scan the street. "And where's Timur?"

Franziska adjusted her grip on the basket of goods from the market. "I don't think he's back yet."

"Would you *please* just be quiet for a moment?" Emma's hushed snip made Antoine and Franziska both take pause, their gaze freezing on her. "While I was at the dock I saw the detective."

Franziska frowned. "Detective Davies? The one who unleashed the hounds on us?"

"Impossible." Antoine shook his head.

"Yes." Emma's eyes widened in fear. "I don't know if he saw me or not. He didn't chase after me so I think we're still safe, although I do think we should get out of here just in case."

"I agree," Antoine replied, spotting Timur making his way through a busy sidewalk across the street.

He motioned for him to hurry and Timur jogged the rest of the way, his perfect chin-length curls bouncing against his dark, angular jaw. All the colour drained from Antoine's face when Timur neared them, grabbing the man's broad shoulder that barely fit around his bicep.

"How could you be so careless?" Antoine asked, grabbing Timur's collar and pointing to the red dot Emma could only guess was blood.

Timur's eyes flashed crimson, sending Antoine a warning. "I was careful. I passed a hospital and only took what I needed."

"Did you kill anyone?" Antoine said in a hushed tone, ensuring no one else passing by could overhear.

"No," Timur growled, shoving Antoine off.

"Stop it, you two. We *need* to leave. Now."

Emma followed Franziska's frozen eyes that were on the taller of the two men walking up the street deep in conversation. Antoine and Timur turned to see what the concern was about and quickly turned their gaze elsewhere, not wanting to draw attention to the detective as he passed them.

"Come along," Franziska whispered, leading the way in the opposite direction, further into the crowded market.

Emma held her breath. Though she desperately wanted to look over her shoulder to see if they'd lost them, she wouldn't risk it. She moved as quickly as possible without drawing attention to herself, falling in step with Timur.

"Did you at least save me some?" she asked, glancing at the others to ensure they didn't overhear her.

The corner of Timur's lips turned upward ever so slightly before returning to his usual straight face, reaching for a vial he'd tucked into the red sash he wore as a belt. It was the one piece of clothing he had from his home and refused to part with it. Or, at least that was what Franziska told her when she asked why he always donned it.

Since the night she'd accidentally eaten Timur's dinner, she'd found that in order to have access to her power outside of the full moon, she required blood. Since then, Timur had been secretly providing her a little bit whenever he could without the Beaumont brothers finding out. She didn't want to prove Artus's suspicion correct that she was exactly what his first impression of her was. That she was a liability just like Timur. And she especially didn't want to give Antoine any more reason to keep her from performing with them.

In return, she agreed to stop asking Timur so many questions. She wondered where he'd come from, how he'd become a vampire in the first place, and what he was hiding from that made him cling to the animal his blood consumption turned him into. He kept a wall up between him and the rest of the circus, but Emma could tell it was just to keep from reliving some painful memory. Those with agonizing pasts could easily spot a kindred spirit.

"This changes everything," Antoine said for the hundredth time since returning to their camp on Deadman's Island. He paced in front of the fire Kizmet lounged beside, the panther's eyes never leaving Artus who lay on his back nearby tossing a rock up into the air.

"Are you sure it was the detective?" Artus asked, throwing the rock even higher.

Kizmet's eyes followed the rock as it arched through the air, skimming a tree branch, before spiralling down and landing gracefully in Artus's other hand.

"Yes." Antoine stoked the burnt kindling from the previous night's fire with a stick.

"We all saw him," Franziska confirmed, followed by Emma with big armfuls of the firewood Timur was chopping up.

Artus threw the rock up again and this time Kizmet leapt over him, catching the rock in his mouth before spitting it onto the mush of leaves and dirt beside him. "What did you do that for?"

You didn't let me play with it earlier, Kizmet grumbled.

Artus rolled his eyes. "Maybe later."

"How will we perform now?" Emma asked, lighting the fire with a snap of her fingers.

"With the detective in town I don't see how we can," Antoine replied.

Artus pushed himself up, resting on his elbows. "So why don't we leave? We aren't even supposed to be here. And don't tell me it's because you've had one of your visions again because I'm sure if we can't work we'll starve."

"There's someone here who needs us," Antoine tried to explain.

Artus caught the look of fear Franziska shared with his brother and scowled, brushing the leaves and soot off and taking a seat on one of the logs surrounding the fire. Absinthe followed, taking her usual spot at his side.

Timur joined them, dropping the last load of chopped wood with the others and taking a seat next to Absinthe. She visibly shifted her paws further away from him.

"I might have an idea," Emma said quietly.

All of them looked at her.

Emma hesitated, building the courage to continue. "When I was out exploring I ran into Mr Dods."

"Who?" Artus asked, tucking a loose strand of his chin-length hair as black as his panthers behind an ear.

"You know, dockmaster who helped us after the *Augustus* crashed."

Antoine let out an ugly laugh that made Emma jump. "That buffoon who couldn't keep his eyes off of my dear Franziska?

"There's no need for that, Antoine." Franziska glanced at him with disappointment.

A small smile crept at the corners of Artus's lips and Emma imagined he was daydreaming of Franziska ending her romantic relationship with his older brother. That would probably be the happiest moment of his life.

"What did he say?" Timur furrowed his dark brows, absently touching his forefinger where a ring might've been.

Emma always did wonder why he did that. "He told me of one place that might be interested in a performance."

"Who?" Antoine demanded, an edge in his tone.

Emma swallowed hard. "Mrs Dolly's Salon."

"Ah, how lovely." Artus clapped his slender hands together. "Isn't that near where we passed through the night we first arrived? What was it… Brunswick Street?"

Antoine's piercing grey eyes grew wide, contrasting with his pinched expression.

"Artus, stop," Franziska warned before resting a hand on Antoine's shoulder, making Artus scowl. "Please, it's not so bad of an idea. Give it a chance."

Antoine shook his head. "I won't condone subjecting you to such a dodgy street."

"It wouldn't be the first dodgy street I've frequented." Franziska shrugged, but this only instigated a fit of loud shouting matches between the two.

Much to Franziska's horror, Antoine forbade her to even set foot on Brunswick Street and Emma's cheeks flushed, hating herself for even bringing the subject up.

No one even noticed when she left the camp, needing to

get away from all of the shouting. It reminded her too much of her old life.

She kicked a rock in her path, watching it scuttle down the little uneven path through the damp forest. The white mist rolled low through the brush, curling up around the tree trunks towards the darkening sky when a sombre ring met her ears.

Stopping in her tracks, she peered through the mist. What kind of bird would make such a noise? The tune sounded again from behind her and she spun around, the path leading back to the camp obscured in the rolling fog. Had she come from that way? Or had she come from her left?

The faint tune drew closer to her, fluttering between notes in a way that couldn't be from a bird.

"Hello?" Her voice was unusually high. They were supposed to be alone on Deadman's Island, so who would be playing the flute in the woods on a deserted peninsula?

Her eyes darted around, trying to remember the direction she'd come from. Her breath catching in her throat when she realised she was completely lost in the thick vapour. How would she ever find their camp now?

A twig snapped from behind and she spun around, facing a giant cloud of mist. A shadow from within it towered over her, drawing closer with every second and she held her breath.

The sudden howl of a wolf in the distance sent a gust of wind rushing through the towering shadow, bursting through the wall of smoke to reveal the giant had only been a rotten tree stump oozing with worms and mites. A squirrel sat, perched atop it nibbling on a piece of bark.

"Oh, hello there," she smiled, laughing at herself that she'd gotten herself so wound up over a little squirrel.

Spotting a tree nut on the ground, she paused, eying the

squirrel carefully before lowering to her knees and scooping it up.

"This'll be a much better dinner for you, little sir," she whispered.

Taking soft, deliberate steps towards the stump, she held her breath as she got closer. The squirrel nibbling the bark suddenly froze, his eyes locking on her and she stopped in her tracks.

She didn't speak a word as the little fellow inspected her. She imagined he was evaluating whether or not she was a friend or dinner and hoped he somehow saw her intentions were pure. After several moments, the little ball of fluff must've decided she was a friend because he went back to his eating.

Taking another step towards the squirrel, the stump suddenly toppled over with a crash sending the little critter flying off of it, scuttling through the brush in the opposite direction.

"Wait! It's all right!" Emma cried, lifting the nut up into the air.

It was too late, though. The squirrel was already long gone.

"Well, that was disappointing for the poor squirrel." A small voice chuckled from behind her.

She spun around at the unexpected voice. She backed up, nearly tripping over the rotten stump when she met the wide-eyed ghost of a teenage boy hovering on the path in front of her.

7
ARCHIE CONRAY

THE LAD FROZE, his translucent body flickering as the faint tune of a flute hummed in the breeze. "You heard me, didn't you?"

A tingling sensation swept up Emma's arms when he spoke.

"Y-yes?" she replied, wondering if she might've hit her head.

"Oh, this is wonderful!" The boy laughed delightedly, the sound of it dull like he was trapped in a box. "You've no idea how long I've been trying to communicate with *anyone*. I've even given chatting with the squirrels a chance, but they're not much for conversation."

He stopped, flushing when he realised he was rambling and gave an apologetic smile. "Sorry, it's just good to finally talk to someone who can actually hear me."

Emma's breath caught when he silently walked towards her, his body shimmering when he walked through the stump. Not even his feet could be heard as he floated over the dead leaves.

"I'm Archie"—the young lad extended his half see-through hand out—"Archie Conray."

"Emma," she finally replied, reaching for his hand only to gasp when hers went straight through his, leaving a cold, damp sensation on her palm.

Archie's cheery expression faltered, staring at his ghostly hand. Wisps of his dark side-swept hair fell into his eyes, evidently disappointed by being unable to shake hands. He quickly shrugged it off. "Do you have a last name, Emma?"

She glanced around, still unable to comprehend how she was talking to a ghost right now. "No, it's just Emma—well, my circus mum gave me the stage name Monique Ambrose, but my real name is just Emma."

She didn't know why she'd just told him all of that. She wasn't used to being around others her own age and she hoped she was making a good impression. Though she was pretty sure he was just a figment of her imagination so what was the harm?

"Monique Ambrose..." Archie pondered the name, stroking the faint beginnings of a goatee coming in on his otherwise youthful face. "It's elegant and I like it, but Emma suits you."

"So you don't think I'm elegant?" Emma narrowed her eyes.

Archie blinked repeatedly. "Er, well no... I mean yes, I didn't mean..."

"I'm teasing you, Archie." She chuckled.

"Oh." He blushed, joining in her laughter. "You said your circus mum gave you this other name... are you *really* in the circus?"

"Why? Do you not believe it?" She turned to continue her walk through the woods once the curious mist dissipated.

"I don't know," Archie said, quickly matching her step,

floating alongside her. "I've never met anyone from a circus. Are they all as beautiful as you?"

A smile played at the corner of Emma's lips and it was her turn to blush. "That's quite forward of you to say."

"I'm so sorry." Archie bit his cheek. "I meant it only as a compliment. It's hard for me not to put my foot in it, being dead and all."

Emma furrowed her eyebrows. "How did you die, if you don't mind my asking? And why are you here, on Deadman's Island? It's quite deserted."

Archie tucked his hands in the pockets of his trousers held up by suspenders, gazing into the distance. "It seems deserted to you, only to me it is very crowded."

"How?" She glanced around the forest. There was no one to be found except for the distant fog.

"Do you know why it's called Deadman's Island?"

She shook her head and so he continued.

"During the war, this little peninsula was used as a burial ground for the dead of a prison camp. Thousands are buried right where you're standing."

The hairs on the back of her neck stood upright as a chill rushed through her body. She swallowed hard, unsure she liked the sound of that.

"Since then, I guess you could say it sort of attracts trapped souls waiting to move on."

"Move on to what?" Emma wondered.

Archie shrugged. "No one knows."

"Why are you trapped?"

"There's something I still have to do, something my living self was supposed to do." Archie grimaced. "I just don't remember what it was... At least that's what Mr Peaton says."

"Mr Peaton?" Emma folded her lips over her teeth. "Sorry, I'm asking lots of questions, aren't I?"

"It's okay, I had lots of them too when I became a ghost."

Suddenly the air whooshed around them, sending Emma's crimson hair flying and Archie's form nearly floated away.

"There you are!" Timur's deep voice made Emma jump.

He'd appeared out of nowhere in front of them, likely from him using the nifty lightning-speed ability being a vampire gave him. Towering over her, his red eyes dissolved back to their usual sorrel hue as the power wore off.

"Timur!" Emma gasped. "What are you doing here?"

"You left the camp and I couldn't feel your heartbeat anymore," he said, his eyes flitting around the forest as if expecting danger.

Emma couldn't help but smile. It meant a lot that Timur would come search for her. It meant he cared despite him telling her once that he'd lost this ability long ago. Though Timur tried to mask his feelings with his bloodlust, she knew he would always look out for his family. She didn't know why Artus gave Timur such a hard time. Yes, it was true he was dangerous and often succumbed to the darkness, yet wasn't she battling the same thing? The temptation of losing herself every full moon to something so evil it gave her nightmares just thinking about it. None of that meant she was a lost cause, and she was determined to believe Timur wasn't either.

"Who's he?" Archie asked, eyeing Timur curiously.

"He's a vampire," Emma replied, "And performs with us as a clown. He's from the Ottoman lands, although he's very secretive about his past."

Timur frowned. "Who are you talking to?"

"It's Archie." Emma motioned towards the ghost beside her, glancing to see that Archie was no longer there. "Archie?"

Emma turned around, peering through the forest trying to find the boy who'd just been here.

She frowned. "He was just here..."

Had it all been her imagination after all?

"Come along. You've been out in this cold too long."

She scratched her head, wondering how she was even able to see Archie at all and a little bit sad that she didn't get a chance to say goodbye. She hoped it wouldn't be the last time she saw him. Promising herself she'd return another time, she finally followed the vampire back down the path to their camp.

"You were worried about me, weren't you?" Emma asked, giving him a side glance and taking note of how he drew his lips into a thin line. She knew she was right even before he responded.

"No."

"Then why did you come searching for me?"

Timur cleared his throat. "I told you. I couldn't hear your heartbeat among the rest of the circus. You know Antoine's rules, we must stay together. He would've sent me to fetch you eventually."

"I knew you weren't just the animal you made yourself out to be when I first met you. I knew you cared." Emma smiled, lifting her chin up. "Does this mean you'll tell me what happened to your ring?"

Timur absently touched the empty space on his forefinger before letting out an irritated growl. "No. And stop asking."

Emma shrugged, certain he'd open up to her eventually. She would just have to be patient.

The Halifax Club on Hollis St

. . .

"TELL ME AGAIN, from the beginning, how you came to find Archie." Wilson sat back into one of the many tufted leather seats lining the wall near the freshly lit fireplace in the main hall of the gentlemen's club.

Barnaby scratched his balding scalp, his knee bouncing nervously and nearly toppling the coffee table between them along with their glasses of gin. "I told you everything I know already. I was waiting on the Fairbanks Wharf for the *Augustus*. Mr Dods was there—"

"The dockmaster you claim hanged himself outside of a pub?"

"Oh no, he didn't hang himself." Barnaby brought the glass to his lips taking a swig. "He was murdered."

"Indeed. Go on."

Barnaby set his glass down. "We shared a few pleasantries, and then the ocean swelled, flashing bolts of purple lightning across the blood-red waters!"

"Spare me the theatrics, dear Barnaby." Wilson rolled his eyes, taking a long draw of his cigar.

"But it's true!" His eyes grew wide. "And then I heard it..."

"This music that tells you something bad is going to happen?" Wilson smirked through the thick smoke billowing up and joining the rest of the haze above them.

"Yes." Barnaby leaned forward in his seat, his gaze never faltering. "Wilson, do you believe in the supernatural?"

"The *supernatural*?" Wilson snorted, slapping his knee with his free hand, shaking his head before taking another puff. "Oh, Barnaby you do amuse me so."

Barnaby slammed his hand down on the table startling a nearby table. He gave an apologetic smile before hardening his gaze at Wilson. "Think about it. How else would you explain the music I hear? And what would cause ducks to just drown themselves? Or ravens to seek the indoors?"

"Or a man who isn't really dead to be hanging in the empty streets?" Wilson raised an eyebrow.

"Exactly! You can't deny it. Especially with Mr Dods being a ghost and all." Barnaby reached into his pocket, retrieving one of the metal boxes from the crime scene. "Look at these marks on the lid."

"Barnaby, you can't truly believe in all that hullabaloo, can you? There has to be another explanation for what you saw."

"Just look at it, will you?" Barnaby pleaded.

Wilson sighed but felt compelled to humour him and took the box, turning it over in his hand.

"That's the one I found on Archie's body. It's the exact same as all the others," Barnaby explained, sitting on the edge of his seat.

He glanced down at Barnaby. "I thought you said the duck march and the lady's cat happened before the arrival of the *Augustus*?"

"Precisely!"

"So then how could Archie be in possession of this box?"

Barnaby let out a puff of air, taking another swig of his drink. "God knows how many times I've asked that question and I've still not a clue."

Wilson pursed his lips, considering the box with a newfound interest. He didn't believe for a second that anything magical had happened. It was understandable, what with Barnaby's loss, that his mind would have convinced himself something otherworldly happened. However, there was only ever ordinary and so Wilson was certain something much more mundane could explain it all. He just had to figure out what that was.

"Who have you investigated so far?" Wilson asked, popping the lid of the box open. He could sense Barnaby's distress when he did so, though he pretended not to notice and grasped the soft velvet pouch, lifting it into the light. He admired the sheen that cascaded across the crimson cloth, the irregular pattern crushed into the nap in a way only a truly skilled weaver could achieve.

"Well..." Barnaby rubbed his hands together, recalling their names. "First there'd be Mr Dods, though I'm not sure how reliable a ghost is, and then there's Mrs Tilcott—you know, the poor woman who lost her cat?"

"Of course," Wilson acknowledged, deciding to ignore the preposterous remark about Mr Dods being a ghost. "On the day you found Archie dead—"

"Murdered," Barnaby corrected.

Wilson sighed. "Yes, murdered, you said you shared pleasantries with Mr Dods. What did you all say to each other? And use your exact words."

Barnaby eyed Wilson warily as he brought the velvet pouch to his nostrils to smell it.

"He asked me who I was waiting for and I told him about Archie and our plans, how I was going to teach him the business. Nothing gory like what you deal with, but for theft cases and such. Practical skills in performing interviews, drawing conclusions, the basic stuff that could be applied to solve any victimless crime."

"Naturally." Wilson took another long whiff of the pouch so loud it made one of the club's butlers stop and take note.

"Gentlemen, is everything in order?" the butler asked, glancing between the two men.

"Yes, everything has been in quite good order." Wilson smiled, pocketing the pouch.

"I'm glad to hear it. Is there anything else you might need? A refreshment of your drinks, perhaps?"

"No, thank you. I think we're both quite all right for now. You've been very helpful."

"Of course, I'm at your service." The butler gave a small bow. "And if you did not get a chance to hear the announcements, we've a new special guest for your entertainment."

"Oh?" Barnaby's countenance brightened. Wilson rolled his eyes, uncrossing and recrossing his gangly legs and puffing his cigar in an attempt to distract himself from the butler's interruption.

"Yes, I believe she is a psychic of sorts," the butler replied. "Madam Onay can be found in the drawing-room if you should fancy a reading."

Wilson suddenly stopped to pay attention. "Did you say Madam 'Onay'?"

The butler nodded.

"Onay… Onay…" Wilson pondered the name. "It's quite an unusual name. You said she's new?"

"She is, sir." the butler replied. "Is there anything else, sir?"

"No, no, that'll be all."

The butler bowed his head before moving on to other patrons.

"So you *do* believe in the supernatural I see." Barnaby grinned.

"Nonsense." Wilson nestled back into his chair.

"But then what was all that about?"

Wilson frowned. "What was what about?"

"*That*! Your inquiry about the psychic!"

"Just satisfying my own curiosity." Wilson shrugged. "You don't hear the name Onay every day. What else did you and Mr Dods talk about?"

Barnaby scratched his head, trying to remember his train of thought before the butler's interruption. "There was some chat about the weather and a few break-ins, yet nothing out of the ordinary. Come now, Wilson, I don't understand why we must go over and over the tragic events. I've told you everything. Besides, we're about to get a visitor informing us the body's been delivered to Doctor Larson's."

"Really? However did you know? Oh, nevermind now, we've got a dead body to examine." Wilson leapt up from his chair, smothering his half-finished cigar in the ashtray before dashing off. "I knew once the initial shock wore off your talents would return!"

"It was nothing so spectacular," Barnaby replied, ambling after Wilson who was quite a bit faster, what with his naturally tall frame and all. "I merely looked out the window and recognised the messenger from the docks."

Wilson didn't pay any of the startled gentlemen staring after them any mind, sprinting to the front entrance to the club and opening the door just as the young lad who helped him with his bags was about to enter.

"So sorry, sir." The young lad removed his ruddy cloth cap, bowing his head while giving a weak smile. "I've just been sent to deliver you a message."

"Yes, yes I know. John, is it?" Wilson said, not giving the boy any time to respond before brushing past him. "Show us to the well-man."

"Er… yes, sir." The young man scratched his messy dishwater head of hair.

He waited for Barnaby to pass before replacing his cap and scrambling to race ahead of Wilson, who was already past the telegraph office about to cross Sackville Street. Barnaby hardly believed anything useful could be discovered from examining the body, aside from ruling out disease or infection as the cause of death, but as he followed Wilson Davies down the bustling streets of Halifax, he prayed, for Archie's sake, that his colleague could discover much more.

8
THERE'S SOMETHING ABOUT THE BRIGHTSMITH

Dr Larson's Office
Bishop Street, Halifax

THE DOOR CLANGED behind Barnaby and Wilson as they let themselves into the doctor's office, entering a small waiting room of sorts with a counter at the far end.

"Hello?" Barnaby called out into the void of the empty room while Wilson gazed about the room with his hands folded behind his back. "I don't think anyone's here."

"Nonsense, the doctor just wasn't expecting us." Wilson swung the little bell on the desk in front of an array of shelves filled with vials of medicine before turning to Barnaby. "That should suffice."

Wilson pivoted on his back heel, motioning for his colleague to follow him through a doorway next to the desk.

"I don't think we should be doing this," Barnaby hissed, following Wilson before he disappeared through yet another closed door.

"Why ever not? We were told to come here. Besides, I can smell the putrefaction of our poor victim."

Barnaby grimaced, his insides lurching at the mention of rotting flesh. He did not smell it at first, but as they neared the last door at the end of a lonely hallway the stench finally reached his nostrils and he quickly removed his handkerchief.

"Doctor Larson," Wilson said as the door swung open.

The doctor jumped, startled at the intrusion, glancing up at them over his spectacles from where he stood behind the one-armed corpse on the examination table. He furrowed his bushy white eyebrows. "Sirs, I must ask you both to leave. I'm not seeing any patients today."

Wilson chuckled. "Oh, that's very silly of you to say. Very silly indeed. We're not here to get a checkup or something for our runny noses, we're here to inspect the body."

Dr Larson blinked repeatedly. "And you are?"

"Have you identified the body yet?" Wilson ignored the doctor, coming to stand beside the table and staring inches away from the dead man's swollen face.

Barnaby cleared his throat. "Doctor Larson, we haven't had the pleasure of meeting yet. I'm Detective Barnaby Grey and this is a colleague of mine, Detective Wilson Davies. A specialist in violent crimes."

"Oh." The doctor's eyes widened, taking a step back from the table as Wilson continued his examination. "Well, despite this being quite unorthodox, it's a pleasure to meet you."

The doctor stretched his hand out in greeting towards Barnaby, who removed his hand holding the handkerchief to shake it only to gasp at the smell, "Oooh!" Barnaby quickly returned the handkerchief to his nose.

"You'll have to excuse Mr Grey here," Wilson replied, straightening. "He's a bit of a gentler nature."

Barnaby rolled his eyes at his friend for teasing him. Wilson winked in return.

"And you are?" The doctor prodded Wilson.

"I'm exactly what Doctor Grey described. A specialist. Now, have you identified the body?"

"Yes," the doctor finally replied, returning his attention to the examination table. "This is Gene McNab. I recognised him right away. He'd been in my office nearly every day complaining about terrible headaches since taking that job up at the foundry a few weeks ago. Such a shame he's dead."

"*The* foundry?" Wilson raised a brow. "I'd assume there's more than one in Halifax."

"Yes, of course," Dr Larson replied. "But none of them are as well to do. Most are going out of business because of them."

"How do—?"

"I reckon you mean Talmage & Sons Foundry on Lower Water Street?" Barnaby inquired safely from the furthest corner from the dead body, his face still tucked behind the cloth.

Wilson glanced between the doctor and Barnaby, his eyes widening. "Ah, I recognise that name. I was just at Talmage & Sons Furniture. Is there any relation?"

"Of course," the doctor said. "The Talmage family own more than a few businesses in town."

"Hmm…" Wilson pondered this for a moment before returning his gaze to the body of Mr McNab. "Barnaby, would you please spare a moment and take a look at this man's neck with me?"

The shorter man in the corner glanced towards the exit before slowly complying.

"Look at the bruising about the neck." Wilson pointed to the deep purple and blue splotches surrounding the throat. "Do the markings look familiar to you?"

Barnaby gasped as the young face of his nephew lying dead in the Halifax Harbour flashed before his eyes and at the same time, a short toot of a flute's high sharp sounded through the air.

"Did you hear that?" Barnaby gasped, clasping his hands over his ears as he glanced wildly around the room searching for the source of the noise.

Dr Larson's eyes narrowed.

"Forgive him," Wilson said, turning towards the doctor. "The detective just lost his nephew. The young lad was aboard the *Augustus*."

"I'm so sorry," Dr Larson said, giving Barnaby a sympathetic smile.

"So, I take it you did not perform the autopsy for Archie Conray?" Wilson prodded.

The doctor shook his head. "I'm not equipped for the number of poor souls lost on the *Augustus*. I believe they were taken to the military hospital for examination."

Wilson clasped his hands together, turning to his colleague. "Well, I think we've gathered everything there is to be seen here."

"Absolutely," Barnaby said, needing no extra prodding to make his exit.

"Sir, there's just one more thing!" Doctor Larson called after the detectives just as they were leaving.

Wilson paused by the threshold while the doctor rushed to his desk beside the examination table, retrieving a tray with various items arranged on it.

"These are Mr McNab's personal effects." The doctor brought the tray to Wilson who immediately spotted the metal box with identical pyramid shapes engraved on the lid.

The doctor eyed the box as Wilson took it. "Ah, such a strange thing to be carrying around. Though, not quite sure what it is, to be honest."

Wilson tilted his head. "Have you seen what's inside it?"

"Yes. It's a peculiar thing, really." The doctor set the tray back on the desk. "However, I'll let you see for yourself. Being a *specialist* and all."

Wilson gave a wry smile before dashing off after his colleague.

"Barnaby, why are you running?" Wilson asked, relaxing into his normal stride next to Barnaby that was much too fast for his old friend.

"I'm not running, I just don't want to be anywhere near that… that ghoul!"

Wilson rolled his eyes at Barnaby's dramatic declaration. "Isn't it curious how Mr McNab died with the exact same wounds as Archie?"

"Yes, very strange."

"And how they both were in possession of a rather unique box." Wilson brandished the metal container he'd just retrieved. "Presumably both toting a crushed velvet draw-string bag of teeth."

Barnaby stopped in his tracks, his wide eyes locking on the box Wilson held. "Have you opened it yet?"

"No, I was hoping you'd do the honours." Wilson stretched his arm out to hand the box to him.

Barnaby quivered, paling at the sight of it. "I'd rather not."

"Your loss." Wilson shrugged, tucking the metal box in his pocket next to the other velvet pouch of teeth. If he collected any more trinkets he would need bigger pockets.

"So whoever killed the brightsmith also murdered my Archie? I don't like this. Not one bit." Barnaby waved a shaky finger up at Wilson. "Whatever's lurking about, committing such atrocities, he's got to be of the supernatural sort. Mark my words, Wilson."

"Someone *is* lurking about, I'll give you that." Wilson motioned for Barnaby to continue their walk down the sidewalk. "But I promise you there's no one otherworldly involved at all. That's just preposterous."

Barnaby cocked an eyebrow. "Oh? Do you have a suspect in mind?"

"More of a profile, although a person of interest has crossed my mind." Wilson folded his hands behind his back, glancing at Barnaby who hung on his every word. "It's odd how an identical metal box to the one found on your nephew's body was also donned by the ducks and Mrs Tilcott's cat before Archie'd even arrived in Halifax, yes?"

Barnaby nodded, mumbling something about it having to be a demon.

Wilson chose to ignore this, continuing with his hypothesis. "So, either our suspect is someone who can be in two places at once, or—"

"Or the murderer is a witch!" Barnaby cried.

Wilson glared down at Barnaby, his patience growing thin. "*Or* someone who was aboard the *Augustus* who also had a connection to Halifax. A partner in crime with connections, obviously that would require someone rather wealthy, *and* someone with unlimited access to the materials and equipment necessary to forge such metal boxes."

Barnaby's mouth fell open. "You don't mean to tell me you suspect that the Talmages had anything to do with the murders, do you?"

"Oh, Barnaby." Wilson clapped a hand on his old friend's shoulder. "That is precisely what I'm telling you. In fact, I believe our next stop should be *the* foundry."

Barnaby let out a terrified whimper as he stepped up the pace to keep up with Wilson. "You can't just barge into people's businesses accusing them of murder with no evidence!"

"I don't have any intention of accusing him outright." Wilson abruptly turned the corner onto Barrington Street. "I only mean to gently prod around and see what turns up. I mean, the Talmage's do fit the profile. Wealthy, deeply connected, and they just so happen to own a metal factory that seems to be the reason so many foundries are going out of business? I say, Barnaby, if that doesn't sound suspicious to you, I don't know what would."

With a determined spring in his step, Wilson darted back across Sackville, only this time, he pushed his way into the loud factory on the corner.

The door clanged shut behind them, their ears drowning in the scraping and shouting of the bustling factory. Wilson wasted no time in locating Mr Talmage's office in the back. He spotted the greying man through the glass window, hunched over his desk, and proceeded to waltz by the secretary guarding the door. The elderly woman sternly tapped against the keys of her typewriter with the precision and intensity of an orchestra conductor. So absorbed in her work, she barely noticed Wilson waltz by. That is until he reached the door handle.

"Oh, sir!" she called, rising from her chair sending the legs scraping against the concrete floor.

Barnaby paused by her desk. "I'm so sorry for the intrusion. Is Mr Talmage available by any chance? We only need a few minutes."

She frowned. "And what is this concerning?"

Before he could reply, Wilson was already halfway inside the office. "Mr Talmage Senior, I presume?"

"I'm so sorry," Barnaby said to the secretary, grimacing before following his colleague.

"Now, wait a minute!" the secretary called after them, pushing her way into the suddenly cramped room.

Mr Talmage welcomed the two unannounced guests with a stiff posture and furrowed brow. "Gentlemen, I don't believe I was expecting a meeting this evening. Did I have you on my schedule?"

"I'm ever so sorry, sir," the secretary quickly replied, "I was just filling the orders like you asked when these two—"

Mr Talmage lifted his hand. "It's quite alright, Mrs Peaton. I can take it from here."

The secretary, evidently reluctant to leave, hesitated by the door as if Mr Tamlage would suddenly change his mind.

"I'm very sorry for your loss, Mrs Peaton. I'm sure your husband was a fine soldier." Wilson bowed ever so slightly in the secretary's direction.

"Wilson!" Barnaby hissed, flushing crimson.

The old woman's eyes bulged, placing a hand to her heart. "Why I never.... how dare you!"

She huffed, glaring between the two intruders before retreating to her desk. The offence she took at Wilson's forthrightness could be heard through the open door as she resumed the clickety-clack of her typing, the staccatos even harsher.

Barnaby and Wilson returned their focus to Mr Talmage whose mouth fell. "Who are you? And how in the world did you know she'd lost her husband?"

Wilson's lip twitched, taking the man's inquiry as a compliment. "A detective never brags, or I should say not usually, but I would be remiss if I did not notice the ring she wears on a chain around her neck that's much too large for her delicate fingers nor the homemade honourary medal on her desk."

"Ah, yes. Such a touchy subject that is." Mr Talmage scratching the back of his head. "She couldn't get the real medal because her husband had already died in the war. She never did remarry."

"Even after thirty years?" Wilson let out a short laugh that was met with an awkward silence. "Yes, well, moving on. I'm Detective Davies and this is Detective Grey. We were here hoping to ask you a few questions about a brightsmith in your employment. A Mr Gene McNab, I believe."

"Of course." Mr Talmage motioned for Wilson and Barnaby to have a seat in front of him. "Has he done anything wrong?"

"He's dead," Wilson replied, sitting.

Barnaby cleared his throat, adjusting his collar.

"Oh my." The many lines on Mr Talmage's forehead creased together as he slumped back into his chair. "I'm very sorry to hear that. He was an excellent metal worker, although a few health issues now and again, but otherwise I had no complaints."

"You seem to know precisely the man I'm referring to." Wilson cocked an eyebrow. "A busy man like yourself, running dozens of businesses in town, and many workers in your employment, I'd imagine much too occupied to know your employees by name."

Barnaby stifled a cry and Wilson rolled his eyes.

"Now listen here, Detectives"—Mr Talmage leaned forward, resting a cuffed sleeve elbow on his desk and wagging his finger at them—"I won't have you coming in here accusing me of anything uncouth."

"*Uncouth*?" Wilson chuckled under his breath.

"We're so very sorry, Mr Talmage, sir." Barnaby was quick to defuse the situation.

Wilson pulled the metal box from his pocket, placing it on top of the unseemly mess that was Mr Talmage's desk. "Have you seen this box before?"

Mr Talmage huffed, furrowing his brows while gazing at the box with a curious focus. Taking one final deep breath, he reached for it with a scowl. Balancing the container in his fingertips, he inspected the workmanship with a trained eye.

The man's eyes widened in recognition when he noticed the strange symbol upon its lid.

"You recognise it?" Barnaby gasped.

"It's a rather unusual trinket." The old man's expression hardened, shrugging as he tossed the box back. "But no, I've never seen that box before. Why?"

"It was found on Mr McNab's body when he was pulled out of the well."

Mr Talmage stood, his face twisting in rage. "I'm not liking where this is going. Now, I've got a lot of work to do and, as you said, I'm a busy man. I want the both of you out of here!"

"Gladly." Wilson rose from his seat, straightening his frock coat before returning the metal box to the confines of his trousers. "We'll be in touch."

Barnaby gave a weak smile, before following Wilson out of the office.

"No, we surely will not!" Mr Talmage called after them.

"How could you be so rash?" Barnaby cried but lowered his voice when he met Mrs Peaton's nasty glare.

"Did you see the way he looked at that box?" Wilson smirked. "He recognised it. I know it."

They retraced their steps through the factory, taking care to keep out of everyone's way.

"Welcome back, Mr Talmage!" A worker called to the gentleman they'd just passed.

Wilson glanced back at the rather tall man, his grey frock coat draped over his shoulder revealing a deep crimson velvet vest with a rather unique sheen to it.

"Thank you, Clyde," the tall man with a thick and stylish moustache greeted.

"Oh!" Wilson turned to address Irvin Talmage Jr when Barnaby quickly grabbed Wilson's arm, yanking him towards the exit.

"Would you let go of me?" Wilson shrugged from his friend's grasp. "Honestly, I don't know why you're so upset. Yes, I may have behaved a bit carelessly, but it was all part of the plan and has made my hypothesis of who the killer is all the more clear."

"And who is it now? Mrs Peaton?"

"Don't be ridiculous." Wilson sighed. "You heard the worker in there, welcoming Mr Talmage's son back from being away. If it hadn't been a long time then he wouldn't have been greeted as such. Also, it's very clever of him to hide his wounded arm he clearly got from the *Augustus* crash with his coat. Although I'm not sure how the Beaumont circus fits into all of this, perhaps Irvin is part of their little gang as well. Nevermind that now, I shall put it all together very soon."

Barnaby frowned. "Mr Talmage's son is now a part of the *circus*? That's preposterous! And I don't see how any of this means he was aboard the *Augustus* or that he's the murderer of two innocent lives, a cat, *and* managed to get hundreds of ducks to just up and drown themselves!"

"Oh, I did forget about the ducks," Wilson said, scratching his bristly chin. "I will have to investigate that further, a work of the circus, no doubt, but Irvin was on that ship. I'll prove it, and when I do, I will be making my case for his arrest and trial."

"You must stop acting with such haste, Wilson, I beg of you."

"What do you mean? I'm only trying to help solve these murders as you asked me to."

"Yes, solve them. Not gallivant door-to-door accusing everyone of murder before getting all the facts and dragging *my* name in the mud while you're at it." Barnaby let his cheeks puff out, unable to hold back any longer. "Don't forget, when you go back home *I* will be here. Relying on these people for work and if you're wrong—"

"I'm never wrong." Wilson lifted his chin.

"*If* you're wrong I will suffer for it. Think of that while you're gallivanting." Barnaby, having had enough excitement for one day, bid his farewell to Wilson and marched in the opposite direction.

"Barnaby! Wait!" Wilson called after him, but it was no use as he was already halfway to Lower Water Street.

He wasn't sure why Barnaby was so upset, it wasn't like he knew the Talmages well, and everything they'd discovered today pointed in their direction. The connections, the father who owned a foundry with the tools to forge the custom boxes, and the crushed velvet vest Irvin Talmage was wearing. The fabric was identical to the material the pouches within the box were made of, he was certain of that. There was very little room in Wilson's mind to fathom anyone else being the killer, and he had the determination to prove it. With any luck, he'd have two murderers on trial before the week was over. The murderer of Barnaby's nephew *and* the butcher's daughter, who he was sure to find at the *Beaumont Bros. Circus's* performance at Mrs Dolly's Salon.

9

FIREWORKS & FRIENDSHIPS

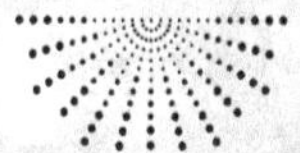

Deadman's Island

STANDING in the open space of grass just beyond their campsite, Emma gripped the slender handles of two juggling clubs with her right hand and the third club in the other.

One.

With a sweeping motion, she flipped the top club in right up, letting it arch.

Two.

She launched the club in her left into the air, catching the one she'd just tossed.

Three.

Before the club from her left fell into her hand, she tossed the last club in her right.

Catch.

She caught the final club, now holding two clubs in her left and one in the other.

One, two, three. She repeated the whole thing in reverse as she continued the rhythm, chewing the corner of her lip. She was so focused on keeping the clubs from dropping that nothing else existed.

"Relax, let them fall to you," Timur advised her when she tried to reach to grab the wooden handle flying through the air.

"Ugh!" She groaned, her mistake sending a wooden club plummeting to the soggy forest floor.

It rolled to Timur, who popped it up with his foot, catching it in hand with ease. "You're distracted."

"I can't help it." She shrugged. "What's the point in practising at all if Antoine isn't even going to let me perform with you?"

His sorrel brown eyes softened, gently handing her the club. "You know this has more to do with the place than it does you."

"But he acts like he doesn't even want me here." Her eyes stung at the thought. "You've no idea what it feels like to live every day like you don't belong anywhere. My parents are dead, and if Antoine decides to kick me out, I'll have nowhere to go."

Timur took a deep breath, closing his eyes for a moment as if struggling with his next words.

"Come"—he motioned for her to have a seat on a fallen tree trunk—"sit."

Her shoulders slumped, sitting on the log next to Timur's towering frame and resting her head in her hands. They sat in silence for several moments, the cheerful staccato of the tree swallows chirping to each other in branches above.

Emma snuck a peek up at Timur, whose gaze was far away, the centuries of lifetimes he'd lived reflecting in them.

"Before this circus," Timur began, drawing in a ragged breath, "and long before either of the Beaumont brothers' time, a cruel and selfish woman once lived behind the veil."

"In the Transitioned World like Artus and Antoine's father?"

Timur nodded. "A terrible greed lived inside her heart, and when she grew unable to live within the confines of her world, she escaped in the shadows."

His voice was soft, barely above a whisper, and she leaned in. She'd never heard him speak about his past like this before.

"This world did not yet know of the evils you call 'vampires'." He grimaced, the unfamiliar word falling oddly from his lips. "But when she arrived in the Ottoman lands, her evil swept through the empire like a plague, turning those she could manipulate into bloodthirsty Ubir. She was our queen, and we were cursed to obey her misdeeds."

He stopped, squeezing his hands into fists as red anger flashed across his eyes.

"Is that who turned you?" she asked.

Taking a deep, calming breath, he shook his head. "I never knew life before becoming this monster. As a child, I was abandoned at a janissary camp to be trained in a secret group of Ubir soldiers. I never knew my parents, what it was to be human, or to have a home until I met Emel... she was everything to me. But not even our love could escape the queen's wrath."

He turned towards Emma, his eyes darkening. "When you put your home in the hands of others it can always be taken away. Best to keep it in your heart."

Timur then stood, picking up his own juggling clubs and practising in silence. His sorrow-filled eyes focused heavenward as he skillfully tossed them to a complicated rhythm. Emma watched in dismay, the weight in her chest even heavier than it was before. Could that be the answer? To never consider anyone or any place one's home?

Tears stinging her eyes, she pushed herself up from the

log, snatching up her clubs, and stomped towards the melancholic clown.

"I think you're wrong." Her voice shook with resolve, adjusting her stance and finding her centre of gravity before picking up where she left off.

One. Two. Three. She began the sequence of juggling the clubs. *One. Two. Three.*

Timur did not respond, but he was listening. His ancient eyes no longer focused on the clubs he juggled with enviable grace and precision, but on her.

"I think you're afraid and you blame everyone else for what you are."

He sidestepped, trying to duck out of her line of sight, but she matched each movement, their clubs moving in unison now.

"You always say that the world is only filled with monsters." The hairs on her forearm stood up as the tingling sensation of static shot to her fingertips, challenging her grip on the clubs. "That it's just a matter of figuring out what kind of monster you are."

One. Two. Three. One. Two Three.

She continued the rhythm until she tossed her third club into the air, letting it arch towards Timur. His eyes widened at the change in pace but copied her movement without missing a beat, passing a club through the air towards her at the same moment.

One. Two. Pass. The rhythm of the throws quickened.

Wooden clubs cascaded through the air back and forth between the two.

One. Two. Pass. Their arms moved to the beat. *One. Two. Pass.*

"This family chose me. They are my whole world." Sparks shot from her fingertips, the blinding light electrifying each club that she tossed. "They *are* my home whether they like it or not and I refuse to be a coward."

She tossed the last club into the air, flexing her fingers.

Pop. Pop. *BANG!*

Suddenly the flying clubs sparkled in shades of pink and yellow before exploding into a million sizzling pieces of glitter. Emma blinked, unsure of how she made this happen. Were her powers growing?

Timur's mouth fell open, the clubs no longer cylinders of hollowed wood, but shattered pieces fluttering to the ground in beautiful smithereens.

"What is going on over here?" Franziska asked, marching over from their campsite. "It sounded like a gunshot!"

She placed a hand on her silver trousered hip, the frills of her matching blouse fluttering in the breeze. Emma sucked in a quick breath of air, too dazed to reply.

Timur met Franziska's inquiring eyes. "I think I might need to make a new set of juggling clubs."

Franziska's arched a pearled white brow, eyes darting between the two.

"Well, I'm glad you're both all right." She shrugged and motioned for them to follow. "Come. Artus has made us some cabbage dumplings."

Emma watched Timur's expression carefully, her heart sinking when he turned into his tent without another word.

A coward? She kicked herself for being so mean.

Why had she said those things? After all the hours Timur had sacrificed to teach her how to juggle that was how she repaid him? By incinerating his juggling clubs, calling him a coward, and making a horrible assumption about him? A knot formed in her belly, the regret becoming unbearable.

I'm such an idiot, she chided herself, sitting next to the firepit Artus tended.

He hunched over the boiling pot, the peppery decadence within it wafting through the air sending everyone's stomachs growling save for Emma's. She'd suddenly lost her appetite. She knew she needed to apologize, but what if she'd offended Timur beyond repair? What if he never forgave her?

Unable to think about what happened anymore, she snuggled in between Kizmet and Absinthe. The clink of tin bowls and spoons in the background was swallowed by Kizmet's loud purr when he placed his head on her lap.

"You will all have to be careful if you insist upon doing this performance," Antoine warned the rest of the group seated around the firepit. "Might I suggest you use your stage names at all times?"

"Is the almighty Antoine asking for our opinions?" Artus smirked, pulling his long black hair into a knot at the nape of his neck before digging into his bowl of dumplings.

Antoine glared at his little brother.

"You mean for a *whole* evening you'll all have to call me Fraulein Mystique?" Franziska winked in an attempt to ease the tension. "I think I can manage that."

Her infectious laughter echoed around the fire, stirring a few countenances to brighten.

"Oh, but Antoine!" Franziska cried, a playful smile tugging at her lips. "Dear Artus doesn't have a name yet."

Artus grimaced. "I've never needed one. It's not like anyone even notices me when there are two panthers on the prowl."

"But Artus, you do have one," Emma piped in, unable to avoid the conversation.

"What? Have you two conspired without me?" Franziska pouted, feigning disappointment.

"No, but isn't it obvious?" Emma grinned. "His stage name is Sir Tygar the Lion Tamer, of course."

Emma jumped when Absinthe groaned, letting her chin flop onto her front paws.

"I know, my sweet," Artus replied to the panther's thoughts only he could hear. "The title isn't entirely representative."

Absinthe moaned again, this time louder.

"What is she saying now?" Emma asked.

Artus rolled his eyes. "She says it's rather presumptuous of us to think I could tame anything."

The whole group erupted in laughter. Their delighted giggles contrasting against the darkness where the ghosts of souls in limbo surrounded them. The conversation moved on, Emma letting it fade into the background as she stared into the dark forest. She'd almost forgotten that they weren't entirely alone until a sudden fog rolled in and, with it, the distant melancholic tune of a tin flute in the breeze. She held her breath and scanned between the trees dancing with fireflies for her newfound friend.

She knew she shouldn't leave the camp without telling anyone, but she couldn't help it. She wanted to see Archie again. What if Antoine found out and forbade her from seeing him? Or worse, force them to pick up and move again? No, for now, she would keep this to herself. She wouldn't give Antoine any more reason not to let her perform.

Hiding behind a tree trunk, Archie's shimmering torso peeked around the corner and waved.

"Archie," Emma breathed, giving a small wave back.

His ghostly shadow flickered in the bioluminescence and motioned for her to join him.

She paused, gazing over her shoulder at her companions absorbed in their conversation and plans for their upcoming performance. Would they miss her if she disappeared for a few moments?

Kizmet noticed her tension and looked up at her, a curious glint in his dark eyes.

Emma brought her forefinger to her lips. "It's okay. I'm just going to visit my friend for a few minutes."

Kizmet let out an abrupt puff of air from his velvety nose.

"You could come with me?" Emma offered the annoyed panther.

Absinthe let out a low rumble, conveying her disapproval.

Emma rolled her eyes. "Oh, please don't worry. We won't be going very far."

Kizmet moaned at his partner's overprotectiveness, looking to Artus for support, but, to Emma's delight, he was too engrossed in Franziska's antics to notice.

"Come on." Emma stood, brushing off the rosewood pink pantaloons Franziska had made for her.

She tiptoed away from the campfire, Kizmet following closely behind, glancing back every now and then as if to question his decision.

"I didn't know if I'd ever see you again," Emma said, joining Archie for a stroll in the dark, guided only by the hazy glow of fireflies.

"I wasn't sure you'd be able to see." Archie grinned, glancing at the nervous panther who trotted a few steps behind them. "Who's your friend?"

"That's Kizmet. He's one of the two panthers that belong to Artus, the lion tamer."

Kizmet hissed. Archie's eyes widened, jerking his attention back to Emma.

Emma bit her lip. "I mean they don't *belong* to him, they're just... part of the circus, but Artus is the only one who can hear their thoughts."

"He can read their thoughts?"

"Yeah, it is a cool power." Emma gazed up at Archie, his

translucent form billowing as he walked. "Do you believe in the supernatural?

Archie tilted his head. "Like in the folktales?"

"Yeah, something like that." Emma shrugged.

"Back home, my mum used to read me these stories about the angels from another world." Archie paused, gazing off as if he were lost in thought before shaking his head in laughter. "But I guess I do believe now, seeing as how I'm a ghost and all."

Emma smiled, halfheartedly. The pit in her stomach returned at the mention of home, reminding her of the confrontation with Timur.

Archie must've noticed as he stopped, peering deeply into her eyes. "What's wrong? Did I say something wrong?"

"No, it's just..." She paused, unable to look up from her feet. They came to halt and she let out a sigh. "I never had parents or a home before the circus. Not really."

"I'm so sorry." A sadness swept across Archie's face.

"No, it's quite all right," Emma said, not wanting his pity. "I love the circus. They're my family. My home."

"But?"

She grimaced. "But Antoine—the ringleader—he doesn't want me to perform even though that's all I've been training for and..."

Her shoulders slumped and she sighed before meeting Archie's attentive gaze.

"I may have taken my frustration out on a friend who's done nothing but help me."

Kizmet must've sensed her distress because he was instantly at her side, abandoning his mission of keeping his distance from the ghost.

"Have you spoken to your friend about it?" he asked, sneaking glances at the giant panther nudging her arm.

She scratched the back of Kizmet ears, stalling as much as

she could. There was no need to respond, though. From the look in Archie's eye, she could tell he already knew the answer.

"You know, I just realised something," he said, gaining her attention. "I never answered your question from before, about how I died."

They continued to walk, keeping just out of sight from the circus's campfire.

"Me and my parents, we didn't always get along"—Archie kicked a pebble in their path—"Particularly with my pa. He always had it in for me to follow in his footsteps, but I can't stand the sight of blood."

Emma furrowed a brow.

"My pa's a physician, not a vampire, or anything." He winked. "But I had another family business in mind."

"Besides your father's profession?"

He nodded. "My uncle is a detective, a master at solving crimes and growing up I always looked up to him."

Emma's eyes widened, coming to an abrupt halt. "A *detective*?"

"Yes, he lives here. The amazing Detective Barnaby Grey. I wanted to be just like him."

She sighed with relief, glad to know her new friend wasn't somehow connected to Detective Davies who was out to arrest her.

"Why?" He frowned. "Who did you think I was talking about?"

"Oh, no one." She smiled, hastily. "Did you at least get a chance to learn anything from him?"

Moisture glistened in his eyes and it was his turn to avert his gaze. "I didn't get a chance. I arrived on the *Augustus* and—"

"You were on the *Augustus*, too?"

He looked back at her in awe. "Yes, my parents finally agreed to let me visit my uncle, but then it crashed and..."

His voice broke and he lifted a shaky hand to his collar. He pulled the fabric back revealing dark, black and blue markings in the form of handprints around his neck.

Emma gasped. "Someone killed you?"

He nodded, kicking another stone away. "Being a ghost... it's so lonely."

"Aren't there other ghosts to talk to?"

"The thing is, the longer you're in limbo the less coherent you become." He grimaced. "That's why, when Mr Peaton's not trying to figure out his own unfinished business, he's been trying to help me."

Emma wished there was some way she could help him, too. But she didn't even know how she was able to see him. How would she be able to help him move on?

"At least Mr Peaton can get the living to hear him," he continued. "That helps a lot. Unfortunately, I haven't figured it out yet. Every time I try to speak to my uncle it comes out wrong. What I'm trying to say is that I'd give anything to be able to speak to my uncle one last time."

He stopped, turning to face Emma. Her chest tightened when she met his sorrow-filled eyes and she suddenly wished she could pull him into an embrace, but his partially transparent form reminded her that he was just a ghost.

"But you can still make things right with your friend," he whispered, his form beginning to fade into the night. "Don't take that gift for granted."

Emma knew in her heart that he was right. Even if she disagreed with Timur, she shouldn't have let her disappointment in Antoine's choice in keeping her from performing out on him. He didn't deserve that. Who knows what kind of loss he'd experienced in his own past to bring him to the belief that one should never trust anyone else? She more than anyone should've been able to understand this reluctance. But instead of showing empathy she'd berated him and destroyed his juggling clubs in the process. She had to make it right, even if Timur didn't think anything of it.

"Thank you, Archie," she said before he vanished completely into the ghostly plane.

Kizmet moaned, nudging her arm to head back to camp. She patted his head. "You're right, Kizmet. It's late. Let's go home."

She followed Kizmet back to the camp, determined to take Archie's advice to heart and make things right.

10
THE KILL OF THE NIGHT

Along the docks,
Lower Water St

Barnaby pushed his stiff legs as fast as he could down the sidewalk. He wasn't sure where he was going, he just knew he needed to put Sackville Street, the foundry, and especially Wilson as far away from him as possible. He'd had enough of Wilson's showy behaviour, gallivanting around and accusing anyone and everyone of being the killer without even considering motive. Why would any of the Talmages kill their own employee? Not to mention, they didn't even know who Archie was and even if they did, who would want to kill his dear nephew? The thought of it stung his eyes and he wiped the moisture away with his wool cuff.

He had no idea how long he'd been walking or noticed that the sun had long since set, his anger fueling him onward along the docks whenever Wilson popped into his mind. It had been a horrible mistake to send word to Wilson. Why couldn't his oldest colleague and friend believe him? He'd witnessed the men hauling the ducks from the water himself and the sight of Mr Dods's dead corpse hanging from a noose in the alleyway would forever be engraved in his memory. And what about the ravens rushing into the Two Crows? He hadn't imagined that Wilson could just ask Tom, after all, he was at the barkeep and would've seen the birds firsthand. Besides all that, didn't Wilson know him well enough to know he wouldn't make any of this up?

Caw!

Barnaby jumped, glancing about the shadows blanketing the street. Only a few street lamps flickered, their dim light playing tricks with his mind. Wings flapped just above his head, and he ducked. The darkness made it impossible to see anything.

When he straightened, the hairs on the back of his neck rose. Someone was watching him. He could feel it. Reaching to adjust his sack coat, he took that opportunity to glance over his shoulder.

His stomach flip-flipped. Did something move?

Frozen on the sidewalk next to Fairbanks Wharf, the sighing waves faded into the background as Wilson listened for any sign of life. A fading light between the buildings illuminated a shadow, sending his thick hands trembling.

"Whoever you are be warned!" His voice broke when the shadowed outline of a large man ducked back into the darkness. "I don't want to hurt you, but I am armed. Please step out!"

The wind howled, fluttering the corners of his collar. His eyes darted about the empty street, but the shadow remained out of sight.

But then, out of the crying wind, what began as a soft whistle rose up until all Barnaby could hear was the anthem of the tin flute.

"No!" He gasped, bringing his quivering hands to his ears,

but it was no use. The tin flute's sombre tune only grew in volume.

Urging his shaky legs to move, he ran further away from the shadow in the hopes that the music would go away. But the faster he ran the faster and louder the flute played until, at the peak of its crescendo, it came to an abrupt halt.

Barnaby stopped in his tracks, wheezing and grabbing his chest as his lungs fought to catch his breath.

Footsteps pitter-pattered behind him and he bit his fist, forcing back a cry. Tears stung his eyes and he was both out of breath and desperately trying to stay quiet. Finally gathering enough courage he turned around to face whoever was following him. He prayed it was only a couple of kids pulling a prank. Hoping for the best but plotting for the worst, he pivoted on his heel.

The empty street flickered in an unnatural red light, illuminating the hourglass silhouette of a woman sauntering out of the alleyway. The ruffles of her gown fluttered in the night's breeze. He sighed, shaking his head and laughing at his own hysteria. The night could do such damage on one's mind, especially with a murderer on the loose. He opened his mouth to call out to her and offer her his arm to escort her back to safety, but when the woman reached the street, he froze in his tracks.

A figure of a large man with beady red dots for eyes appeared behind her, the shadow Barnaby thought was just his own imagination stepping into the light. Dark curls framed an angular jaw he recognised from the day he'd found his dear nephew murdered. It was the dock labourer who'd vanished as soon as he tried to point him out to Mr Dods. A scowl crept across his face, realizing there was, indeed, something supernatural afoot. But how could he prove it?

"Stop!" He cried, but it was too late. The dark man

grabbed the woman, smothering her screams in his giant palm while the other pinned her against him.

Barnaby balled his hands into fists with every intention of fighting this monster but stopped when the man's lips parted, revealing sharp fangs sliding over his canines. He blinked several times, hoping it was just imagination, but then the monster plunged his fangs into the poor woman's carotid artery with surgical precision, leaving no room for doubt.

It wasn't Irvin Talmage or the circus responsible for the murder of his nephew and the brightsmith. He was certain the murderer was right in front of him, the dock labourer from the Ottoman lands, and he was hunting the citizens of Halifax.

The Dockyard,
Upper Water Street, Halifax.

Wilson Davies pulled his pocket watch from his vest, checking the time. It was nearly sunset, but surely he had enough time to get to Upper Water street if he left right then. He looked down Sackville Street where Barnaby had disappeared, wondering if he should go after him, but then shook his head. It was probably best to let Barnaby have a moment to himself. Without a second thought, he set a quick pace towards the dockyard where he was certain he'd find the answers he needed. Irvin Talmage was on the *Augustus*, and he knew how to prove it.

It didn't take him long at all to get through the dwindling crowds closing shop from the market and soon he passed the last wharf, turning into the dockyard. Rows of sea ships lined the yard, the darkening sky nearly disappearing in a sea of white masts. Even at this hour, there were many sailors collecting their cargo from the ships and shouting to dock labourers.

Wilson scanned the crowd, catching sight of a ruddy cloth cap he recognised bobbing behind a huge crate. It belonged to the dock labourer who'd escorted him to Barnaby's.

He cleared his throat, approaching the worker. "Young man, do you happen to know where I can find Mr Dods?"

The metal wheels of the crate screeched to a halt. The lad peered up from underneath his torn cap revealing a scar below his left eye that was impossible to look away from. It made the hair rise on the back of Wilson's neck.

"He's just in there." The dock labourer pointed to a nearby framed building made entirely of clapboard.

"Of course, thank you." Wilson tipped his top hat bidding farewell, before rushing from the horrific sight. What had happened to cause such a terrible disfigurement?

Shaking the thought from his mind, he entered the small warehouse, scanning the cluttered office before spotting the stout dockmaster working on paperwork behind a small desk.

"Mr Dods."

The greying man jumped, nearly toppling the wobbly desk he hunched over.

"Do you have a moment?" Wilson asked, removing his top hat and coming to stand in front of the startled man.

"Man alive!" Mr Dods coughed, turning pink. "Don't ye know not to sneak up on an old man like that?"

Wilson frowned. "I merely entered your place of business, but never mind that, I'm here to see the ledger from the *Augustus*."

Mr Dods set down his ink pen, narrowing his eyes at Wilson. "What ye want with it.?"

"I merely want to see who was aboard the ship when it arrived in Halifax Harbour the day Barnaby's nephew was murdered."

The man's eyes widened. "Ye think the murderer was on that same ship?"

"I know he was. In some capacity, at least. So, do you have it?"

"Yes, yes, just wait right there." The greying man heaved himself from his chair, ambling to a nearby cabinet of drawers.

Wilson drummed his fingers against the silk rim of his hat, letting his eyes wander about the bleak office. Other than the lamp on Mr Dods's desk, a single-window angled towards the harbour was the only source of light. It cast a dusty haze through the cramped space. The rows of shelves scraping the low ceiling only accentuated the need for a good tidying. When the last time anyone gave it a dusting?

Mr Dods shoved the wooden drawer closed with a snap, forcing Wilson's attention to the ledger in the dockmaster's calloused hands. "The *Augustus*, eh? Well, here ye go. Although I'm not sure what good it'll do. Most of the passengers on that ship perished."

"Well, in that case, this ledger should be more than helpful." Wilson returned Mr Dods's blank stare with a smile before inspecting the list. He trailed the rows of names with his index finger, searching for any last names beginning with T. "Kildare, Finnerty, Delagney—good heavens, don't you alphabetize?"

"I take the names as they come," Mr Dods said, gruffly.

Wilson pinched the bridge of his nose before continuing his search, holding back the desire to explain what an atrocious lack of organization this filing 'system' was. If one could even call it that. It wasn't until he got to the name 'Onay' scribbled in the margins that he halted his search to read the passenger's first name.

"Secil Onay," he whispered, wondering if this could be the psychic employed by the Halifax Club who went by the name of Madam Onay. Or was it just a mere coincidence?

"What did ye say?" Mr Dods asked his bushy brow wrinkling.

"It's nothing." Wilson looked up, noticing how the stout man's hands began to shake at the mention of the name Onay. "Do you know this woman?"

He pointed to the name on the ledger, but the old man refused to look directly at it. Mr Dods fiddled with something stuffed in his front pocket, a blanket of sweat streaming across his brow.

Wilson pursed his lips, returning his gaze to the ledger. "It's surprising how similar this name reminds me of one introduced to me at the Halifax Club."

"Oh?" The old man removed a shaky hand from his pocket to grab his kerchief from the top of his desk.

"Probably just a coincidence." The detective glanced up in time to catch the dockmaster dabbing the moisture from his forehead. Why would the mention of the psychic at the gentlemen's club make him so nervous?

Finally reaching the last few lines of names, Wilson spotted the one he'd been looking for. IT was barely discernible in Mr Dods's sloppy script which made Barnaby's look like the work of a calligraphist, but there it was. A smile crept across his face when he read the name Irvin Talmage, Jr. He now had his proof that Irving was, indeed, on the same boat as Archie Conray. It wasn't a motive, but it was a connection. He was sure he'd be able to figure out 'the why' once he spoke to Irvin Talmage in person.

Wilson finally handed the ledger back to Mr Dods. "Thank you, good sir. I'm much obliged."

Spinning on his heel and replacing his hat atop his head, he was about to leave when, out of the corner of his eye, he spotted Mr Dods remove what he'd been fidgeting with from his pocket. A crimson pouch identical to the one found on the brightsmith's dead body. Reaching for his coat pocket, he let out a sigh of relief when he felt the sharp corners of the box still tucked away unscathed.

"Sorry, but where did you get that?" Wilson asked.

The man jumped once again, the pouch slipping from his grasp and scattering its contents of sugary rose squares all over his desk. Wilson frowned at the unexpected sight. Instead of a bag full of teeth, it was filled with sweets. The citrus tang of lemon mixed with sugar wafted through Wilson's nostrils.

"It-it's Turkish Delight, sir," Mr Dodes mumbled, unable to make eye contact. "Secil Onay always gives them as a parting gift after her readings."

"So, the woman on this ledger is the psychic after all? How interesting."

"I meant Madam, it's *Madam* Onay!" Mr Dods paled, realizing there was no use in covering his slip. "She's not the killer, of course."

"Of course not." Wilson turned the doorknob, waving his farewell to the disgruntled dockmaster.

Of course, he knew it was ridiculous that Madam Onay was the killer. But he couldn't deny the coincidence. Perhaps she was working in tandem with Irvin Talmage somehow. Either way, he made a mental note to pay this psychic a visit the next chance he got.

11
THE SPECTACLE OF A GENTLEMAN

THE MORNING CAME LIKE A THIEF, stealing Wilson from his sleepless night. He'd tossed and turned, the worry of Barnaby's absence keeping him too alert for sleep. The old man hadn't made it back to the flat last night and with the state they'd left things in, it made Wilson fearful. Particularly with a killer on the loose. What if his old friend was lying in a ditch somewhere? The thought of that made him absolutely livid.

"Stop it," he ordered himself, chastising his reflection in the boudoir mirror for being so irrational. He was probably just with Tom sobering up at the Two Crows. There was no need to worry himself.

Taking one last look in the mirror to tuck a stray lock back into his meticulously combed hair, he made his way out into the brisk Canadian morning. Wilson bounded down the front steps of the building and strolled along Grafton Street, past the soap factory, and onto Prince Street. Welcomed only by a few pedestrians and the crisp breeze blowing in from the harbour, Wilson made it to the front entrance of the Halifax Club on Hollis Street with ease.

"Good day to you, sir," the butler said, taking his frock coat.

Wilson drew in a deep breath, taking in the intoxicating aroma of freshly mopped floors. Pure cleanliness. It made him regret not taking up rooms here, but to slight his dear friend like that would be improper.

"Do you require a table?"

"Oh, no thank you." Wilson smiled politely before marching towards the dining hall. He already had a table in mind.

Upon entering the large, window-lined dining hall, the clink of silverware against the china-filled plates of eggs benedict welcomed him. But not even the buttery perfume of fresh biscuits could divert the detective's attention. He scanned the tidy rows of white-cloaked tables, some occupied while others stood idle awaiting their next guest in the epitome of order. Quiet murmurs mingled between sips of steaming coffee. Then, seated in the back row of tables, the familiar face stood out amongst the rest of the breakfasting gentlemen.

Straightening his solid black vest, Wilson approached the foundry's son. "Mr Talmage."

"And do bring a fresh pot." Mr Talmage said to the waiter, waving him off before turning to the detective who took the vacant seat opposite him. "Good morning. You must be the infamous detective."

"That's quite astute of you," Wilson replied. The unwavering eyes staring back at him conveyed a respectable amount of awareness he would not have expected from the average person.

"Nonsense." A crooked smile curled the corners of the young man's well-groomed handlebar moustache. "My father told me I should be expecting you and, please, call me Irvin."

"Wilson Davies, pleased to meet you." The detective didn't

bother extending a hand in greeting, opting for a menu instead.

The smug expression plastered upon Irvin's face expressed that he expected nothing less from the detective. The two quietly contemplated their next move, sizing each other up until, finally, Wilson chose to break the silence.

"Well"—Wilson snapped the menu shut, tucking it underneath the folded napkin—"I won't insult your intelligence by pretending you don't already know why I'm here. I have questions for you as a man of the law, I suggest you answer them honestly."

"Naturally."

"You're aware of the ducks that drowned themselves in the harbour, are you not?"

"Yes, I heard about that. Quite awful."

The waiter returned, removing the old pot of coffee and replacing it with a fresh, steaming one.

"Your father recognised this." Wilson removed the metal box from his coat pocket, placing it on the table in between them.

"Did he now?" Irvin didn't even look at the box, spooning sugar into his coffee mug before pouring the dark nectar.

"It was found on the body of Mr McNab," Wilson prodded, narrowing his eyes when Irvin refused to look up from his coffee. "He was murdered while under your father's employment, although, with your memory, I'm sure you already knew that."

"Yes, I did hear the news of the brightsmith's untimely death." Irvin's voice remained smooth, but the slightest quiver at the corner of his mouth revealed the subject did not sit right with him.

Wilson also noted how Irvin referred to the deceased as 'the brightsmith' instead of using his proper name—which of course Irvin knew because he knew everyone employed by his father by name and addressed them as such—which Wilson inferred as a subconscious desire to disassociate himself from the victim.

"An identical box was found on the bodies of the suicidal ducks," Wilson continued when Irvin made no attempt to further the conversation. "Do you know what's inside them?"

"I've not the faintest." Irvin took a delicate sip of his coffee.

"A drawstring pouch made of a rather unique fabric." Wilson unlatched the metal box, revealing a sheen of crimson cloth. "You can see the crushed pattern of the velvet is rather unique."

"Oh?"

"The vest you were wearing yesterday, it was made of the same fabric." Wilson huffed, growing tired of the young man's vague responses. He had to break him, he needed to push him to reveal the truth.

Irvin squinted with a hard smile, resting his mug gently on its saucer. "I'm failing to see the point here. Are you accusing me of something or simply paying me a compliment for my sense of fashion?"

"The former." Wilson clenched his teeth. "Were you about the *Augustus* when it crashed?"

"Yes."

"Why?"

"For business." Irvin leaned forward, resting his elbows on the table and folding his hands.

"And while aboard the *Augustus,* did you encounter a young man by the name of Archie Conray?"

"Please, Mr Davies." Irvin glanced about the room as Wilson's raised voice stirred unwanted attention from the other patrons.

"Detective," Wilson corrected.

"*Detective*." Irvin rolled his eyes. "You're embarrassing yourself and, quite frankly, speaking to the wrong person."

The tall gentleman stood, taking a clean damp towelette brought to him by their waiter.

"I'm most certainly speaking to the right person." Wilson rose. "And don't you want to know what's inside this velvet pouch that 'just so happens' to be made of the same fabric as your unusual vest? Or wait, you probably already know because you're the killer."

Shocked gasps and wide eyes flooded the expressions from the patrons at tables within earshot.

Irvin threw the used towelette onto the table, his unwavering eyes locking onto Wilson's as he took a threatening step towards the detective.

"You forget yourself, *detective*," Irvin hissed, his face twisting in hatred. "I won't repeat this again, but I am not your killer, and if you defame my family name again, you will be hearing from my lawyer."

"Is everything all right, Mr Talmage?" the butler asked.

The young man scowled back at Wilson before replacing his expression with an innocent smile, turning to the butler. "It is indeed, Victor."

"Shall I ask him to leave for you, sir?" The butler asked, giving Wilson a patronising glare.

"I hardly think that's necessary." The innocent smile upon Irvin's face deepened, an evil glint in his eye. "Just a difference of opinions. Right, *detective*?"

Wilson pursed his lips, hating the idea of agreeing with this grotesque man. But he finally relented, giving him a curt nod.

"There, it's all settled." Irvin took his coat from the butler, whistling as he marched towards the exit.

Wilson closed the lid to the metal box before quickly following him. "But then where did you get the vest?"

Irvin paused by the door. "It was a gift."

"From whom?"

The young man sighed. "From Mrs Tilcott for watching her cat while she was away."

"As the heir to a great fortune, that does surprise me."

"I take pride in caring for this town," Irvin replied. "Not even the smallest task is beneath me."

"How kind of you. However, poor Mr Whiskers is dead."

"Then take this up with Mrs Tilcott, because that is as much as I know." Irvin secured his light grey bowler hat on top of his head before bidding him good day, pushing through the double door exit and disappearing behind it.

"You forgot this," the butler said, begrudgingly handing him his frock coat.

"Oh, thank you." Wilson reached for it before turning to leave.

He was about to head out when a familiar voice echoed from behind the grand staircase on the opposite end of the front entrance.

"I'm forever in your debt, Madam Onay."

Wilson frowned. The quivering voice reminded him greatly of Barnaby. Ignoring the butler's insistence that he take his leave, the detective marched towards the voices, passing the doors to the cigar lounge and dining hall. The voices grew louder when he stepped closer to the source, around the mahogany staircase into the hallway behind it. A cracked doorway revealed a woman with long, dark brown hair, deep olive skin, and hazy emeralds for eyes. A matching green bandana was tied around her forehead, a golden jewel dangled from it and hung between her brows. Wilson held his breath, taking a step closer to see who she was speaking to, and his eyes fell upon the back of Barnaby's sack coat.

"Thank you for everything." His colleague's voice broke,

looking down at his shaky hands that the psychic had grasped between hers.

The woman smiled, leaning forward and planting a gentle kiss upon his cheek. "Be well, dear Barnaby, and blessed be."

Wilson fumed, unable to decide if he was more upset that Barnaby hadn't come home last night or that he'd been consorting with a psychic of all people.

"What's going on here?" The detective marched up to the two, their heads jerking towards him when he neared.

"W-Wilson!" Barnaby stammered. "What are you doing here?"

"My job, dear Barnaby," he replied, "the better question is where have you been *and* what are you doing here with her?"

"Detective Davies." The hazy-eyed psychic suddenly lurched towards Wilson, grabbing his arm as her irises rolled back into their sockets. "He's close... the murderer has been watching you."

"Unhand me!" Wilson yanked his arm from the psychic, her eyes returning their focus.

"Has the killer really been watching us?" Barnaby asked the psychic as a jagged tooth grin spread across her face.

"Come, we've much work to do." Wilson didn't have time for the spectacle this woman was causing, guiding Barnaby away as quickly as he could.

"Be careful not to play his game!" Her cackling laughter echoed behind them as they left, leaving goosebumps crawling up his arms.

"What were you *thinking*?" Wilson growled once they'd made it out onto the sidewalk along Hollis Street.

Barnaby turned on Wilson, forcing them to a halt. "I was getting answers. You've no idea what I saw last night."

Wilson frowned. "What could you possibly have seen last night that would keep you away from the flat at all hours of the night? I was worried sick about you."

"I'm sorry for that, but last night"—Barnaby took a deep breath, on the verge of hyperventilating from all the excitement—"our killer killed again, but this time I *saw* him."

"You saw Irvin Talmage commit murder? Well, then why aren't we arresting him?"

"That's just it, it wasn't Mr Talmage."

Wilson rolled his eyes. "Of course it was, he recognised the metal box—the same as his father—and he was on the *Augustus*. I verified it with Mr Dods's records."

Barnaby shook his head. "It was someone I'd seen before. Not Mr Talmage, but a dock labourer I'd noticed moments before the *Augustus* came crashing through the harbour."

His increasing volume awarded them a few disapproving glances and he quickly lowered his voice to a mere whisper.

"I was up all night with the police, but none of them saw the killer as I did. I tried to explain it, but I had no idea how. It was a nightmare. A mere shadow until the man flew at the woman illuminated by a lamp and dug his teeth into her neck. I recognised him..." his voice cracked, gazing off into space.

"Barnaby, get ahold of yourself. This doesn't make any sense. Are you *sure* that's what you saw?"

Barnaby quickly nodded. "It was the dock labourer who vanished when I pointed him out to Mr Dods. It was he who killed the poor woman."

"But you said he bit her?"

"Yes. Madam Onay explained everything to me," Barnaby continued. "She says in her country it's known as an Ubir, although this one has seemed to evolve into a form that resembles more of a man than a demon."

"A what?"

"An Ubir. A demon that survives on human blood. It's a vampire!"

Wilson swallowed hard. A pit formed in his stomach

when a memory of the crime scene he'd walked into at a pub in London popped into his mind. Each victim had punctured wounds along their carotid artery. Wilson shuddered, remembering the horrid stench of rotting corpses and the rivers of blood flowing from their necks. Later, under the influence of much tonic, he'd convinced himself that what he'd seen that night was all in his imagination. It had to be stress or something. But was it?

He shook his head at the foolish idea. "Vampires don't exist."

"But they do!" Barnaby insisted. "I knew something supernatural was happening, I just couldn't see what it was until now. Madam Onay says he'll be at the circus's performance tonight at Mrs Dolly's Salon."

"Even if I did believe in vampires, which I don't, your nephew and the brightsmith were strangled, not drained of blood."

"It's him. I know it is," Barnaby rambled on, ignoring him. "It's that foreign dock labourer. He's the vampire and he's part of the circus. Madam Onay foresaw him at the show."

Wilson rolled his eyes, about to scold him for believing in such things when a shrill scream from around the corner gained their attention.

"What was that?"

"I don't know, but we'd best find out," Wilson replied, motioning Barnaby to follow him.

They ran the short ways to the corner of Hollis and Prince, stopping in their tracks when they approached the source of the commotion.

Barnaby gasped. "Who is that?"

"Everyone, stay back!" Wilson warned, approaching the disfigured body in the street. A sense of dread gripped him when he spotted the light grey bowler hat on the ground near the front wheel of a horse-drawn bus.

The sidewalks became congested with pedestrians stopping to look or consoling each other. Children and women were pulled from the bus, shielding the little ones' eyes from the horror that lay just on the other side of the vehicle.

"Whoa, there," the driver tried to soothe the upset horses.

Wilson stepped out of their way, his stomach rolling when he approached the body sprawled unceremoniously across the brick-laden street and meeting the vacant stare of Irvin Talmage, Jr.

12
TURKISH DELIGHT & THE CHASE

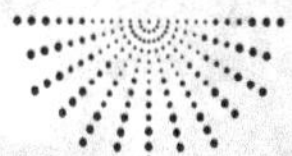

A SUDDEN RINGING in Wilson's ear drowned out the shouts and cries from the passersby. He didn't understand. Irvin Talmage was the killer, he had to be. But now he was dead. How could this be?

Wilson blinked, his vision clouding. He'd been so certain.

"You're embarrassing yourself." Irvin's smug voice filled Wilson's mind as he replayed his last words. *"I am not your killer."*

He grabbed his head, squeezing his eyes shut as Madam Onay's cackling voice joined in Irvin's mockery.

"The murderer has been watching you." Her cloudy emerald eyes flashed in his mind. *"You're playing his game!"*

Her chilling laughter echoed around him, paralyzing him until, suddenly, a firm arm gripped him.

"Wilson."

He snapped his eyes open meeting Barnaby's.

"Are you all right?"

Wilson shook his head, rubbing his eyes. "Yes, quite all right."

He pushed passed Barnaby, ignoring his friend's concern, and knelt in front of Irvin's body to examine it.

"Let me through!" A frantic voice cried from behind them on the crowded street corner. Not an inch of sidewalk could be seen.

Wilson tried to ignore the deafening shouts, taking note of the deep, blood-red splotches lining the whites of his eyes. Then the black and blue impressions about his neck. All the signs of it being the same killer as the first two murders.

I thought for sure it was him. Wilson cursed himself. He'd been so focused on Mr Talmage that the real killer could've been right under his nose and he wouldn't know it.

"Strange," he murmured to himself.

"Hmm?" Barnaby asked, only glancing in his direction, but keeping his eyes safely averted from the dead body.

"There are fresh markings on his neck." Wilson pointed to the carotid artery and a chill ran down his spine. "Our killer couldn't have gone too far. But how did no one see the killer?"

"It's a vampire!" Barnaby's revelation crept into his thoughts, but he quickly disregarded it. That idea was not only improbable it was quite preposterous.

But then how could he explain the two gouges in the side of the late Irvin's neck?

"That's my son!" Mr Talmage cried, pushing his way through. His hands shook uncontrollably when he spotted Irvin. "What have you done? Take your hands off my boy!"

The elderly man launched himself towards them.

"Barnaby, could you please?"

"Of course," Barnaby replied, stepping in between the frantic Mr Talmage and Wilson as he resumed his inspection of the body.

The whistle from the police officers sent most of the pedestrians scattering.

"My boy," Mr Talmage whimpered, falling limp against Barnaby.

"It's all right, sir." Barnaby attempted to console the older man crying on his shoulder.

Wilson gave Barnaby an appreciative nod when they caught each others' glance before continuing his investigation.

"The bruising pattern is the same as the brightsmith's," he announced, gaining Barnaby and Mr Talmage's attention. "There's just one last thing we must find that will assure me Irvin's killer was the same."

The old man sniffled loudly, still clinging to Barnaby. Wilson ignored Mr Talmage's relentless sobs, sifting through the dead body's clothing for the metal box. He reached into the pockets of Irvin's light grey trousers, coming back empty. He padded the man's chest, seeing if there were any signs of something in his vest, but, still, those pockets were empty. Then he moved on to the man's frock coat, reaching into the inner pocket.

"There you are," he muttered, retrieving an identical metal box with interlocking pyramids on the lid.

"What's that?" Mr Talmage asked.

"This, my good sir, is proof your son and your employee, Mr McNab, were both killed by the same man."

"Or demon," Barnaby blurted in a hushed tone, loud enough for only Wilson to hear and roll his eyes, but quiet enough that it only prompted a quizzical frown from Mr Talmage.

There was something different about the way Irvin looked now than he did before. Aside from the bloodshot eyes and bruised neck, of course. His cheeks were much too puffy.

He snapped his fingers. "The killer's left us a message!"

"A message?" Barnaby's eyes bulged. "How?"

Wilson gripped the man's jaw.

"What're you doing?" Mr Talmage cried, pushing away from Barnaby about to tackle the detective.

"Stay back," Wilson ordered, lifting a hand up.

"Please, Mr Talmage," Barnaby tried to reason with the distraught man. "We need to examine the body to determine more about the killer."

"I think it's clear who that is." Mr Talmage glared at Wilson. "It's *him*! He came to my shop accusing me and my son when really it was Detective Davies all along."

Barnaby's wide eyes narrowed, turning livid. "Now, listen here, Mr Talmage—"

"Aha!" Wilson exclaimed, prying Irvin's mouth open.

"What is that?" Mr Talmage gasped, distracted by what the detective was doing.

Barnaby turned just as Wilson lifted a chunk of something pink and powdery from Irvin's dead mouth.

Barnaby gagged, bending over at the waist when Wilson sniffed the partially chewed substance.

Whiffs of lemon and rosewater met Wilson's nostrils and he gasped. "Turkish Delight."

Mr Dods's words popped into his thoughts. *"Secil Onay always gives them as a parting gift after her readings."*

A sudden chill swept through Wilson's body at the memory. "But that's not all that was left."

Mr Talmage frowned. "What else did you leave, then?"

The detective ignored him, lifting Irvin's top lip to get a better view of his gums.

"What happened to his teeth?" Mr Talmage cried.

Wilson sighed. What he could decipher from the crime scene defied all reason, but he couldn't deny the evidence.

"I've got an inkling the killer removed them and stuffed them in here." Wilson raised the metal box he'd retrieved from the body.

"Aaack!" The splash of Barnaby's vomit echoed behind them.

Wilson unlatched the metal lock on the box, lifting the red velvet pouch and tugging on the drawstring revealing the missing teeth.

"See?" He straightened, handing the pouch to the astounded businessman.

A sudden tingling sensation at the nape of Wilson's neck alerted him that they were being watched and, with it, a low whistle hummed in his ear. He shook his head, popping his ears in the hopes to alleviate the noise, but it was no use.

He scanned the sidewalks, trying to ignore the tin flute clanging in his head. If this was the music Barnaby had been complaining about, he now understood why. It grew even louder as he evaluated each spectator until it came to a screeching halt when his eyes landed on a pair of emeralds staring back at him.

"It's her," he breathed.

A sly grin spread across Madam Onay's face before turning, running back down Hollis Street towards the gentleman's club.

"Come, we must stop her!" Wilson pushed his sapphire-clad feet into a full sprint, slapping Barnaby on the back when he raced by.

Barnaby stood upright, wiping his jaw on his sleeve.

"Wait up!" he called, but Wilson was already bounding up the club's steps after the psychic.

Pushing through the doors, the butler cut off his line-of-sight. "I'm afraid you're not welcome here, sir."

"Not now, Victor!" Wilson shoved the startled butler aside, catching a wisp of the psychic's frilled skirt disappearing behind the staircase.

I've been watching you. Madam Onay's sing-songy voice

echoed in his mind, but of course, this had to be his imagination.

He raced after her, bumping into anyone and everything in his way. His heart pounded in his ears as he ploughed through the door into the empty drawing-room. For a second panic gripped him. Where did she go?

Barnaby's heavy tread finally caught up to him just before he spotted the flutter of a curtain directly to their left. He darted around the round table, bumping the corner of it sending the glass ball rolling off the side and across the room.

"Please, you must slow down!" Barnaby huffed when Wilson pulled the curtain open revealing a narrow passageway.

I like it when you think you're onto me. The psychic's cackling laughter returned.

"Stop it!" Wilson cried, turning a corner just as she disappeared through another door.

"Who are you talking to?" Barnaby shouted after him, following the two through the swinging door and stumbling onto a bright-lit platform. An auctioneer stood on the stage next to a vase placed on a pedestal out on display for the gentlemen occupying the seats that lined the front row.

"Next up, this gold-encrusted—" the auctioneer stopped, an incredulous stare plastered on his face.

The psychic flew off the stage, aiming for the doors in the back. Wilson spared no delay. Jumping off the stage, he quickly gained on her.

She glanced over her shoulder, pushing herself even faster.

Wilson's foot caught on something and he grunted, stumbling forward.

"So sorry," a young lad said, scooting out of the way.

The door clanged shut, distracting Wilson from registering the boy.

"Carry on!" Wilson called, leaving stunned attendees in his wake.

He thrust the door open, stumbling from the auction house onto a bustling sidewalk on the backside of the gentlemen's club. He scanned for their pursuant between the carriages rolling down Granville Street, spotting the psychic's wild hair from the crowd.

Catching a break between the traffic, he darted across. He grinned, finally within arm's reach of her, when the psychic suddenly turned. Her emerald eyes locking on his before rolling back into their sockets making Wilson slow down.

You think you're close. Madam Onay's voice deepened in pitch, no longer resembling a woman's voice and growing louder in his head. *But we're just getting started.*

The corner of her lip curled in a devilish grin, raising her hand slowly and with a snap of her fingers she vanished. Wilson screeched to a halt, his mouth falling. That wasn't possible. People couldn't disappear into thin air. But no matter how many times he blinked, the space Madam Onay once occupied remained vacant.

Barnaby let out a throaty cough, hissing and wheezing for air when he finally caught up to him. "Did you…ahh"—he bent over, resting his hands on his knees, attempting to get control over his breath—"Did you see that?"

"I…" Wilson paused, not wanting to vocalize what he'd just witnessed.

"She vanished, just like magic," Barnaby declared, way too cheerfully for Wilson's liking. "It's supernatural, that's what."

"Stop it."

"And I bet you she's right after all." Barnaby came to stand next to Wilson, padding him on the back.

He sighed. "Right about what?"

"The vampire did it, of course." Barnaby giggled with delight. "And we can catch him in the act tonight at Mrs Dolly's Salon just like she said."

Wilson let out a moan. "How many times do I have to tell you that vampires don't exist? And how can you be so happy right now?"

Barnaby's laughter deepened, his eyes watering which just made Wilson all the more livid.

"Oh, Wilson, I'm just relieved," he said once his laughter subsided. "Magic is real. It's real and I'm not mad after all"—Barnaby tightened his fists, his voice darkening—"and now Archie's killer will hang."

Wilson ground his teeth as he bit back the snide retort he desperately wanted to spew at Barnaby for being so gullible. It was a trick. He didn't know how or why, but it had to be.

13
THE NIGHTMARE

Deadman's Island

Emma woke with a start, her heart pounding in her ears. She had no idea how long she'd been sleeping, but from the rays of light seeping through the flap of her tent, it had to be nearly midday. She gripped her chest, taking deep breaths trying to forget the horrors of the nightmare that had welcomed her last night.

She'd been running from Detective Davies down a dark alleyway. A fog blanketed the ground, curling around her ankles obscuring her path. A pair of red eyes blinked at the end of the alleyway, but it wasn't what made her stop in her tracks. It was the bodiless shadow floating behind the eyes. Then the music hummed, the tin flute still ringing in her ear, jolting her awake. Something was coming. She could feel it.

Her body tingled, a glow emanating from her fingers as she fed off the beaming sun trickling in. She squeezed her palms shut, extinguishing the energy.

Then she gasped, an instant dread washing over her as she remembered what she was supposed to do. "Timur!"

She'd tried to speak to him last night, but he'd already gone to bed when she'd returned to the firepit. At least no one had noticed she'd left. She was certain she'd bee in trouble if they had.

Pushing through the folds of her tent, her gaze darted around the empty campsite. The ashes in the firepit were still steaming, a bowl of porridge left on the stone untouched.

"Where is everyone?" she whispered, clutching her arms to her chest.

Had they left without her? The back of her throat ached, her head spinning at the thought that they might've deserted her. She hadn't even had a chance to say goodbye or set things right with Timur. Blinded by her watering eyes, she didn't even notice the caravan parked behind the tents and the voices of her companions.

"Ah, you're finally up."

The sudden crunch of footsteps on the rotting leaves behind her made her jump. She spun around, meeting Artus's striking green eyes, his long black hair tied back into a knot at the nape of his neck.

She sighed with relief. "You're still here."

"Of course, we hardly need to arrive hours early." Artus picked up the bowl of porridge, handing it to her on his way to corral the panthers. "You should eat."

She didn't even register the bowl in her hands, turning back to him. "Have you seen Timur?"

"I haven't, not since last night," he called back before whistling to Absinthe and Kizmet nearly invisible in the dark forest they frolicked. "Come on, loves. It's time to practise."

Kizmet let out a loud rumble, leaping over the brush lining the surrounding woods. His shiny black coat glistened in the morning light.

The painful ache in her throat returned and she rubbed her suddenly cold arms. It happened again. She'd driven Timur off the ledge and now he'd probably gone and lost control after all this time. Why had she been so afraid to speak with him when she'd had the chance? She kicked herself for being so cowardly, storming back into her tent and smothering her head in her pillow.

She was about to drown her sorrows in the tears that stung her eyes when hushed voices past by the outside of her tent.

"Why would you let him go?" Franziska whispered to the second pair of footsteps.

"It had to be him," Antoine's voice replied.

Emma sat up, scooting closer to the tent's walls so she could hear them better.

"Don't tell me, because of your vision?"

Antoine made no response and from Franziska's exasperated sigh, Emma inferred he must've nodded.

"Franziska, you have to understand. I can't see what happens tonight, this darkness, whatever's coming, it's blocking me somehow."

Emma let out a quiet yelp, quickly covering her mouth and holding her breath. Praying they didn't hear her. Remembering the shadow from her dream, she realised she wasn't the only one who sensed something sinister was afoot.

There was a brief pause before Antoine continued, "I sent Timur to scout out this place to ensure everyone's safety."

"But you know Timur's struggle. What if he slips?"

"That was a risk I was willing to take. I won't be there tonight to protect you."

Franziska scoffed. "What makes you think you'd need to? I can take care of myself."

"I don't doubt it," Antoine replied, "but you'll be performing, Artus will be ensuring his cats stay in check, and I'll be here watching after Emma."

At the mention of her name, Emma balled up her fists and stormed out of her tent. "Why can you not see that I don't need to be looked after?"

Franziska and Antoine gaped back at her.

"I need to be free to perform alongside you, to be truly one of you, but you keep treating me like I'm some helpless child." Her muscles quivered as lightning zigzagged across her eyes, the hum of electricity building up in the palm of her hands. "But you fail to protect Timur from himself. You let him go out there by himself and"—she gulped back a sob—"after what I said to him... he'll... oh, it's all my fault!"

No longer able to hold back, the moisture rimming her eyelashes spilt over and streamed down her flushed cheeks.

Franziska raced to her side, wrapping her arms around her in a protective embrace. She whispered soothingly in her ear and rocked her until her tears quieted. The slender contortionist stepped back, gently placing her hands on either side of Emma's face.

"Listen to me." Strays of snowy white hair escaped the confines of the silver and turquoise top hat she donned. "You are one of us. Don't you ever forget that."

Emma blinked repeatedly, trying to stifle the tears that threatened to spill once again.

"And as for Timur." She lowered her hands, rubbing her forehead. "I don't know what was said to him, but if he should give in to his own weakness and throw his whole life away that would be *his* choice. It would never be your fault."

"But I... I called him a coward."

The corners of Franziska's thin lips twitched, her porcelain face cracking as if she thought it was funny. "I'm sure the irony was not lost on him. He's been alive for centuries. If he's not old enough by now to let what you said go then I'm not sure you'd have anything to apologize for."

"I don't even know why I said it. I guess I just didn't want what he said to be true."

Emma wiped her eyes giving a halfhearted nod, but knowing she wouldn't be able to rest until she'd spoken to Timur anyway. "When will he be back?"

Franziska gave a patient smile. "I'm not sure. Antoine?"

They turned to their suit-clad ringleader whose knuckles were turning white from gripping the rim of his black silk top hat so tight. "Not until the end of the show. Come, we need to pack."

Emma frowned. "Pack? Why?"

Antoine did not wait to explain, heading to the tents with a hammer in hand.

Emma looked to Franziska for answers and she shrugged. "He doesn't know what's coming, but senses we will have to move soon."

"It has to do with the darkness, doesn't it."

Franziska's eyes widened. "You heard that?"

"It's been in my dreams. This shadow."

"And what does it do in your dream?" Franziska asked with a tone of wonder.

"It doesn't really *do* anything." Emma looked up at Franziska. "It just sort of floats around nearly unseen. But I get a sense like it has more control over those who are near it than a shadow should."

A silence fell between the two as Franziska looked to Antoine, who was using the claw side of the hammer to remove the tent stakes.

Emma gasped, seeing the unsaid flicker across her eyes. "That's why he doesn't want me to perform, isn't it? Tell me. What has he seen?"

Franziska sighed, turning to her. "Trust me, you will perform with us. Perhaps not this time, but once it's safe and the detective's off our back, you will join us once and for all."

It wasn't the answer she was hoping for, but the resignation in Franziska's voice told her it would be the only one she'd receive for now.

"We won't be able to keep your performing skills hidden for long," she called over her bare shoulder, her asymmetrical suit jacket glittering in the light when she made her way to help Antoine.

Emma took a deep breath in, praying it would all be okay. She would just have to be patient, just like she had to be patient and wait until tonight to get everything she wanted to say to Timur off of her chest. Timur was her friend, and she wouldn't be able to rest until she made things right.

Barnaby Grey's flat,
Grafton Street.

Up before the first foghorn gonged, Wilson had already dusted the chimney, swept the floors—twice—and was now stooped over a fresh steaming cup of coffee by the grimy opened window he could never quite make clean. He'd done everything he could think to distract himself from what he anticipated would be a horrific day of convincing Barnaby that the supernatural and all things involving magic were simply figments of the imagination and otherwise didn't exist.

He pinched the bridge of his nose before taking a sip from his mug. A seagull squawked from the street below, gaining Wilson's attention as it pecked at a breadcrumb along the sidewalk. He watched the white-feathered fellow with envy. His was such a simple world. One that made sense to the seagull. If anything it could not comprehend got in its way, he would just simply fly away and all the little seagulls and their friends would continue on.

"Good morning." Barnaby yawned, pushing through the curtain door and stretching his arms. "Is that coffee? I think I shall join you."

Wilson arched a brow. "What, no 'where's my cigarette case' or 'why've you gone and bloody moved my precious cigarette case?"

An unbecoming smirk spread across Barnaby's face, swinging his arms as he marched to the kitchen.

"Well, aren't we cheery this morning." Wilson nestled back into the wingback armchair, quite certain it was the best purchase he'd made out of all the furnishings he'd acquired for the flat.

"I *am*, aren't I?" Barnaby whistled, reaching into a cupboard and grabbing a fresh mug. "It's the first morning I've truly felt at ease in quite some time and I owe it all to you."

"Nonsense, I didn't do anything."

Barnaby scoffed. "Of course you did. You not only whipped me and my flat into tip-top shape but if it weren't for you I'm sure I would never leave this space again and we'd never have caught the killer."

"We *still* haven't."

"Not yet, anyway." Barnaby took a seat on the footstool next to the piano, his knees rising awkwardly above his waist. He chuckled, raising his mug in cheers. "Perhaps, I ought to invest in another chair."

Rap, tap, tap.

Barnaby jumped, nearly spilling the contents of his mug.

"Expecting company?" Wilson asked.

Barnaby shook his head, his eyes widening. Wilson went to the door and opened it just when a harried Mr Dods was about to knock again.

"Detectives!" he cried, rushing inside the apartment. "I was hoping I'd find ye here."

"Mr Dods, are you all right?" Barnaby rose from his seat, setting his mug aside to greet their unexpected guest.

The stout old mad shook his head, his voice quivering. "I-I'm afraid not."

"Well, I'm sure that's to be expected under the circumstances." Barnaby winked.

"What?" Mr Dods frowned, looking to Wilson for answers who shrugged.

Barnaby rolled his eyes. "Oh, don't play coy. I know what you are, although I'm not sure how you managed to knock on the door, that's beside the point, which is—"

"Oh, this should be good," Wilson muttered to himself.

"You're a ghost!" Barnaby sent his hand into the man's bulky shoulder, expecting it to shimmer through. He frowned when his fingers just hit the greying man's firm arm.

"Are ye mad? I ain't a ghost," Mr Dods growled. "But I might soon be."

"What do you mean?" Wilson leaned forward with sudden interest.

Barnaby's mouth remained open, gaping at Mr Dods as if he expected him to walk through a wall at any moment even though the dockmaster was entirely alive.

"I found this on my stoop this mornin'." Mr Dods brandished a crushed-velvet pouch, identical to the one he'd been eating Turkish Delight from.

From the copious sweat dripping from the old man's brow, Wilson could only assume the contents of this particular pouch were less savoury. "And what does it contain?"

Mr Dods's lip trembled. "A tooth."

Barnaby let out a high-pitched whimper, the colour draining from his face.

"*My* tooth." Mr Dods opened his mouth wide. The space where his grubby canine should've been was just a mess of burgundy flesh. The poor man winced, shutting his mouth and massaging his jaw.

"I think I will need my cigarette case after all." Barnaby disappeared into his bedroom behind the curtain, re-emerging moments later taking a huge draw of his cigarette. He offered the case to Mr Dods who gave a desperate nod.

"Thank you," Mr Dods replied, once they'd all settled into chairs around the table with mugs of coffee in one hand and puffs of smoke billowing from the cigarette in the other.

"So, tell us what this is all about," Wilson prodded.

"I should've come to you sooner, I think, but"—Mr Dods took a deep breath, his thumb drawing circles around the rim of his mug—"after I saw Mr Talmage's son in the street and his teeth I knew I couldn't remain in my denial."

"Denial over what?" Wilson asked while Barnaby remained in silent observation.

"That I'm going to be murdered," Mr Dods cried. "I went to visit Madam Onay at the club, ye see. She told me how it'd be done."

Wilson groaned, rubbing his forehead. "Not you, too."

"Shh, let him speak," Barnaby said, awarding him a glare from Wilson. "Go on."

Mr Dods glanced between the two men, before continuing. "She said I'd be in this dark room behind a curtain like the back of a stage. Music played in the background and had these bruises about my neck. She said a bag of teeth was in my pocket, just like with Mr Talmage!"

He shuddered, his hands too unsteady to hold his mug, and he crumpled back into his seat.

Barnaby gasped. "Did she say what kind of music?"

Mr Dods frowned, taking a puff of his cigarette. "She said it was this hollow sound… flute-like… she said it gave her the chills just listenin' to it. But that wasn't all."

The stout man bit back a sob.

"There was a man with the red eyes standin' next to my dead body." Mr Dods clutched his chest, unable to look away from the velvet pouch placed at the centre of the table. "She said he was responsible. Then I find this bloody bag on my front stoop and my *tooth*! How could someone just rip it out like that without me wakin' or bleedin' all over?"

"It's a sign!" Barnaby replied.

"A sign of what?" Wilson asked. "That an ordinary person would make anything up for money?"

"Don't you get it?" Barnaby stood, darting for his sack coat by the door and rummaging in his pockets. "I saw those same pair of red eyes the other night. It's a vampire."

Mr Dods choked on his coffee. "A *what*?"

"The killer is a vampire. Aha!" Barnaby brandished a folded piece of paper from his pocket. "I didn't believe my eyes, but then I visited Madam Onay and she described it all to me."

He returned to his seat, a gleam in his eye.

Mr Dods tilted his head. "You went to see Madam Onay, as well?"

"Yes, isn't she marvellous?"

"You can't be serious!" Wilson's head fell into his hands and moaned in frustration, but the gossiping men ignored his outburst.

"Indeed, she is," Mr Dods said. "But tell me more about this vampire? What's it a sign of?"

"It's not so much the vampire as it is the music." Barnaby slowly unfolded the paper. "You see, I've been hearing this tin flute since the duck incident. When anything bad happens, it returns, and on one occasion it occurred when"—he paused, his forehead wrinkling—"I saw you hanging. From a noose outside of the Two Crows after, you know, the after the *Augustus* crashed and—"

"And ye'r nephew." Mr Dods nodded, looking down into his mug.

"Yes, and also this." Barnaby ironed the wrinkled paper out on the table so that the dockmaster could read it. "I found this in your pocket, the advert about *The Beaumont Bros. Circus* and their contortionist performing tonight."

Mr Dods shrugged. "I've never seen that before."

"I think it was a sign. A vision of the future and your death," Barnaby continued. "Madam Onay said that we'd find the vampire tonight at this performance and if what you say is true, then I believe you'll be the vampire's next victim."

"It's not a vampire!" Wilson snapped, sitting up. "Despite both of you buying into this woman's tall tales, I'm afraid I must bring you back down to the real world. The supernatural just doesn't exist."

Barnaby lifted his chin. "We both saw Madam Onay vanish. It was broad daylight, and there were no trap doors anywhere. Can you explain this?"

Wilson opened his mouth, but then quickly shut it. The corner of Barnaby's lip curled into a victorious smile.

"Whether you believe it or not, the nature of things has shifted." Barnaby turned to Mr Dods. "We shall have to keep you here while Wilson and I go and make the arrest at Mrs Dolly's Salon."

The greying man let out a heavy sigh. "Oh, what I wouldn't give to see Mrs Dolly one last time."

"Get ahold of yourself," Barnaby snapped. "You will have many other opportunities to see her *after* we capture this vampire. Agreed?"

Mr Dods nodded. "But how will you get the beast?"

"Not to worry yourself with that, Mr Dods," Barnaby said, thrusting his shoulders back. "You leave that to Wilson and me."

Wilson cringed. The day had barely started, and it was already turning out to be his worst nightmare.

14
DAZZLING ENCOUNTERS

Mrs Dolly's Salon,
Brunswick Street

Shadows danced in the flickering light as the last rays glistened over the top of the Citadel, reminding him of his brief conversation with the lookout. To put it delicately, he'd been less than helpful.

The cobblestone street echoed with footsteps and the delightful murmurs whispered among friends. Gentlemen clad in their evening best mingled with those less debonair. For one night only, the usual pubs they frequented were passed over for the silver-ribboned entrance of Mrs Dolly's Salon. With tickets in hand, a queue began to form down the pub-lined street for the show of a lifetime. It would seem not a single man in all of Halifax would miss the dazzling performance of the circus's contortionist. Some merely out of curiosity, while others waited in attendance for another reason entirely.

Detective Wilson grimaced, straightening his tuxedo

jacket and glancing about the crowded street. "You never mentioned anything about needing a ticket for entry."

"Don't worry," Barnaby replied, standing poised in a matching three pieced tuxedo, save for the bright pink vest.

Wilson couldn't even look at it without cringing. Barnaby said it was for good luck, but even he'd put up his sapphire shoes for proper evening wear. Anything else would be improper.

"Ticket, please?" the striking woman asked once they'd reached the front of the line. The blonde hair left loose framed her heart-shaped face, bouncing in perfect waves.

Barnaby could hardly respond, his eyes drawn to her hourglass silhouette accented by the silk rose corset.

Wilson cleared his throat, nudging his suddenly mute colleague.

"Yes, my apologies, miss," Barnaby said, snapping out of his daze. "My name is Detective Grey, of course, *you* can call me Barnaby, and my associate, Detective Davies."

Wilson gave a closed-mouthed smile both polite with an air of impatience.

"How do you do?" The woman's singsong voice sent a boyish smile upon Barnaby's lips.

"We don't have tickets. We're detectives, you see, and we were informed you might need added security." Barnaby glanced at the lengthening queue of restless gentlemen awaiting entry.

"Oh." The woman's eyes widened, following Barnaby's gaze. "Did Mrs Dolly send for you?"

"Yes," Barnaby replied.

"Well, then you best go in." The woman quickly opened the door, the boisterous laughter from within growing louder.

A knowing grin spread across Wilson's face. Though he disapproved of Barnaby's conviction that the killer was a vampire, in fact, he'd only come here tonight to prove to him wrong, Wilson couldn't help but be impressed with this man's resourcefulness.

"And the name's Prudence," the woman said, stepping closer to Barnaby and whispering sweet nothings upon his ear.

Upon entering, the two gentlemen were welcomed by a butler who took their coats before moving through the small entry into the main salon. A clink of a glass mingled with laughter and the notes of a lively band welcomed them. An audience began to fill the seats facing a large, red-curtained stage.

A group of gentlemen crowded around the bar, basking in the presence of a scantily clad bartender. Her bustled skirt was hiked so high Wilson was certain he saw a bit of bare thigh above her stockinged knee.

"So, boss," he asked, facing Barnaby once they'd acquired glasses of gin. "How did your 'psychic' say this vampire would appear? Perhaps from a cauldron on centre stage?"

Barnaby sighed. "You still don't believe in vampires?"

"What could possibly persuade me?"

"I thought perhaps seeing Madam Onay vanish like that would be enough." Barnaby brought the glass to his lips. "But then, I'm certain we'd be having a different conversation right now if you'd seen what I saw that night the vampire attacked that poor woman..." He shivered, taking a sip.

"I highly doubt it." Wilson turned towards the stage as the tune the band played changed.

The upbeat staccato of the violin changed to a low mysterious drawl and the lights dimmed. A single spotlight shone on the woman who'd taken up centre stage.

"Good evening, gentlemen," she said, her appealing voice drawing the crowd's attention.

She wore a noble, bustled gown fashioned to mimic a

gentleman's tuxedo, but instead of a proper jacket, her arms were left bare, awarding her a cacophony of whistles and applause. Wilson noted that, despite the efforts made to make herself appear youthful, the air of sophistication in which she carried herself coupled with the salt-and-pepper hair tucked underneath her bowler hat, that she was much older than the rest of the women present.

"Tonight, prepare yourselves for an evening of enchantment, seduction"—she brandished a single white feather tucked between her bosom underneath her black corset, tossing it out into the clambering crowd—"and, for one night only, the dazzling Fraulein Mystique!"

Applause erupted throughout the audience and the velvet curtains drew apart. A woman stood with a baroque-like posture, as still as a statue and as pale as the four-foot-wide fan of white feathers she held covering her slender physique. Her white hair pinned in curls on top of her head glowed in the spotlight. Silver paint dusted every bare inch of her, blending into the tightly fitted corset and high cut trousers briefly revealed when she manoeuvred the feathers to the beat.

For a moment Wilson found himself captivated by her graceful movements. She swayed to the slow, alluring tempo hypnotizing the crowd.

She sashayed across the stage like a gazelle. Each leap into the air or flutter of the fan revealed more of her agility. Balancing on one foot, she rose up onto her tiptoes while the other leg extended painfully high. She didn't even grimace when the leg she lifted reached her shoulders.

A flirtatious smile spread across her face. Twirling the fan she held in front of her, she gave the audience a glimpse of her body contorted into a standing split. This awarded her another round of applause.

She winked, the beat changing as trumpets sounded and

drum rolls quickened. Two men dove out from either side of the stage, their identical black uniforms and masks blending in with the stage's backdrop.

They somersaulted on the ground just behind Fraulein Mystique before lifting a long and narrow board. Hoisting either side of it onto their shoulders just as the contortionist tossed her fans out of the way, letting them fly like wings. She flung her body backwards, hands overhead, arching in a series of back handsprings until she launched her body into the air, spiralling up above the board.

Landing on the centre of the deathly narrow flexible beam, she feigned a fall, hands flailing as her body leaned over the side of it. The men in black sidestepped in unison, dipping the beam propped on their shoulders, catching her fall.

So magnificent was the show before him, Wilson nearly forgot to look for the striking red hair of the butcher's daughter. But Emma wasn't among the three on stage. Was this even the same circus?

But then, in between leaps into the air, their eyes locked. Familiar ice-blue irises sparkled behind silver-tipped lashes and, despite her twisting into bizarre knots each time she jumped from the springing beam, he knew this had to be the woman from the *Beaumont Bros. Circus*. She and her partner, wherever he was, protected the girl on the run for the murder. But now he'd finally get a chance to put this case to rest.

He leaned back into his chair, getting comfortable to enjoy the rest of the show. He was certain Barnaby's vampire theory wouldn't take long to disprove and he'd have plenty of time to question this woman afterwards.

"Get out o' my way," a gruff baritone from the entrance pulled Wilson's attention away.

Wilson drew in a long, irritated breath. “I think we have a bit of a problem.”

He nudged Barnaby, gaining his attention and motioning towards Mr Dods just as he pushed his way past the butler.

Barnaby flushed. “What’s he doing here? He was supposed to stay at the flat.”

Wilson shrugged, crossing his leg. He removed a slender pipe from his pocket, striking a match and lighting it.

“Psssst!” Barnaby hissed, trying to get Mr Dods attention when he walked by their table.

The wide-eyed dockmaster glanced their way, but had no intention of stopping, Barnaby stood, grabbing his arm before the old man could run away.

“Why are you here?”

Mr Dods drew himself up as tall as he could manage. “Makin’ sure Mrs Dolly’s safe. If somethin’ perilous is to happen, I had to come.”

“The only thing *perilous* that happens tonight is your death,” Barnaby spat with a mocking edge.

Wilson his smirk behind a sip of gin.

“Which is precisely why we instructed you to stay put.”

Mr Dods side-glanced to the tuxedo-clad woman from the beginning, mingling with a few gentlemen not paying attention to the circus performance. “And there’s nothin ye can do to stop me.”

He yanked his arm free, marching towards the salon’s elegant proprietor who was now on her way backstage. Realizing they would have to follow him, Wilson took one last puff of smoke before joining Barnaby in pursuit of the dockmaster.

ONCE FRANZISKA HAD SAFELY DISMOUNTED, Artus and Timur bowed before disappearing backstage. Franziska remained in the spotlight, swaying her hips as she teased the crowd, taking the opportunity to slow her accelerated heartbeat. A crimson fabric fell from the ceiling, secured above while the bottom skirted the stage floor.

She glided across the stage to where the silk hung and twirled her arm around the fabric, a splash of red against her white skin.

Impressed murmurs and whistles echoed from the sea of black she faced. Counting to three, she hoisted herself up, tucking her feet on either side of the silk and scaling the ribbon until she was nearly at the top.

Gasps and murmurs echoed from the audience. She grinned to herself, certain they'd never seen the likes of such a performance before.

The music faded into the background. Her breath the only beat she moved to. She swung her body around and above her head, her legs parting as she wrapped the silk around her. With her legs high above her head, she lowered them letting them arch until they bent so far back that they touched the top of her head. Her body formed a circle as she reached an equilibrium high above the audience.

Blood rushed to her ears, her body dangling dangerously high as the silk fabric swayed. Despite all of this, she wasn't nervous. She'd done this routine a million times before, and no matter how many times she twisted her ankle or dislodged her bones, they would always piece themselves back together in minutes.

She untwisted her body, bringing her legs back under her. She prepared to pull herself up even higher on the silk curtain, but an earth-shattering scream from backstage sent her grip loosening. What was that noise?

The audience gasped when she plummeted towards the

stage floor, but she quickly tightened her grip, stopping her free fall a foot from the ground. She stifled a cry of her own when her shoulder snapped against the pressure, dislodging from its socket.

Gentlemen flew to their feet, applauding vigorously, completely unaware that anything was amiss.

Sweat dripped from her brow but she fought the urge to wipe it away. The ringing in her ears was the only distraction from her throbbing shoulder she concealed behind the edge of the silk.

She glanced towards the backstage where the scream had come from, but neither Artus nor Timur were there. She closed her eyes before plastering a smile on her face.

Taking a bow, she ended her routine prematurely, rushing off the stage before they noticed her injury.

"What was that?" Franziska asked, spotting Artus as he stood from where he sat behind a row of stage levers and ropes he used to spot her ribbon routine.

"I've no idea." Artus frowned, eyeing the shoulder she cradled.

"It's nothing," she said before he could ask.

She grimaced, stretching her arm over her head and rotating it until it popped back into place. The black bruises under her silver-painted skin quickly faded back as she healed. She pushed past him, her eyes darting about the darkened space.

"Where's Timur?"

Artus blinked, shrugging.

She took a deep breath, balling her hands up into fists before flexing them. "You were supposed to keep him within sight at all times!"

Harsh voices followed by several footsteps drew their attention to the curtained-off corridor leading to the dressing rooms. They ran for the curtain, running side-by-side towards the dressing room they were assigned.

"NO!" A voice sobbed, followed by a loud thunk.

Shoving the door to the dressing room open, a sudden coldness swept through Franziska's body when they entered.

There, in a pool of crimson blood, Mrs Dolly's lifeless form lay at Timur's feet.

15
THE ARREST

"WHAT HAVE YOU DONE?" Franziska gasped, her eyes growing wide.

Timur swallowed hard. "Fran, I—"

"Ge' out o' my way!" A gruff baritone shouted, shoving his stocky frame between Artus and Franziska.

The greying man froze when he spotted the body, his eyes glistening. He swayed slightly before falling to his knees next to the body. The room filled with his painful sobs.

Timur held up his hands. "I-I didn't do this."

Artus glared, resting his hands on either side of Franziska's shoulders. "It was only a matter of time before you snapped. Now you've put us *all* in danger."

"I promise I didn't kill this woman!" Timur's voice shook, begging them to believe him. He glanced down at the body, furrowing his brows. "I've been keeping it under control since the last full moon. Emma, she's helped me. You know you've noticed a difference."

Franziska shook her head as tears rimmed her eyelids.

"It should've been me," the greying man wept over the body.

Timur's heart sank, realizing what it must've looked like to them. He would've thought he was guilty, too. He'd only come in here to apply a fresh coat of powder to his face. Then, out of nowhere, a ghostly figure shimmered next to his reflection in the light-framed mirror. When he'd turned, the ghost was gone and the woman was already dead. But how could he prove it?

"It's you," another man gasped from the open door frame.

They all turned just as two men entered, gallantly clad in silk black tuxedos.

"You're the vampire," the shorter of the two declared, staring straight at Timur.

"You've been discovered?" Artus frowned, meeting Timur's gaze.

He shook his head, but it was no use. It was clear by the disappointment in their eyes that they didn't believe him.

"Get ahold of yourself, Barnaby," the taller, spindly man scolded. "Go alert the officers. We'll need to clean this up."

Despite the dark, short-trimmed beard, recognition washed over Franziska and Artus's faces. Standing within a few feet of them was none other than Detective Wilson Davies.

"I saw him on the wharf just before the *Augustus* crashed," Barnaby hissed, turning back towards the dressing room door. "He was with that docker but vanished in thin air. That's him, I know it!"

"Yes, yes, now go." Wilson sighed, his nostrils flaring in irritation as Barnaby disappeared through the door.

Franziska looked to Artus. "What did that man say? That he saw Timur *before* we'd even arrived in Halifax?"

Artus only shrugged.

"That's impossible," she whispered, but there was nothing she could do.

The three circus members jumped at the detective's

sudden laughter. Wilson's face flushed, clutching his chest as bouts of amusement tormented him.

"After all this time," Wilson sighed, wiping the tears with a kerchief. "I've finally caught up to you. Granted, I do wish the young redhead was with you so the officers could arrest her as well, but you shall do."

He carefully stepped a gangly leg over the pool of blood and removed a pair of handcuffs from a hidden compartment in his jacket. Yanking Timur's arms behind his back, the metal rattled as he secured them about his wrists just as Barnaby returned with the uniformed police.

"I didn't do this," Timur whispered, his eyes locked unwavering on Franziska. Begging her to see through them and know his innocence.

"There he is." Barnaby pointed, directing the officers to the muscular man Wilson confined in handcuffs.

A few of the officers struggled to separate Mr Dods from the body while others brought in a stretcher to tote it off to the doctor for the autopsy.

"Good work, detectives," one of the officers said, tipping his custodian helmet to both of the tuxedoed gentlemen before turning to Timur. "I'll take this scum from here."

The officer grabbed Timur's shackled wrists, taking care in pressing the harsh iron into his skin.

Timur bit back a snarl. He tossed a curly strand of chin-length hair from his eyes, taking deep breaths to tame the anger that rose from the pit of his stomach. He licked his throbbing gums where his fangs threatened to cut through.

He couldn't react. He could risk letting the beast out no matter if he was being wrongfully accused. He'd made a promise to Franziska, to Emma, and to Antoine who, despite all of his weaknesses, believed in him. Emma had accused him of being afraid and he would do his best not to prove her right. His muscles quivered, straining against his will to remain in control.

He willingly let the officer push him towards the door. "You are under arrest for the murder of Mrs Dolly."

"And for the murder of the foundry owner's son, Mr Irvin Talmage, Jr," Wilson added, cleaning the residue from the handcuffs off of his hands before tossing the handkerchief aside.

"And my poor nephew, Archie," Barnaby growled, spitting at Timur.

"Blimey, how many people has this man murdered?" The officer shook his head, giving Timur another shove.

"He's not a man," Barnaby snapped. "He's an Ubir. A vampire."

The officer's jaw dropped, looking to Wilson for guidance.

Wilson merely shook his head. "Figuratively speaking, of course."

"Ah," the officer replied.

Before Timur disappeared with the officer, Franziska whispered in his ear. "Stay calm, I believe you. I'm going to get Antoine, he'll know what to do."

Timur gave a single nod, a slow smile playing at the corners of his lips. Relief washed over him, and he remained complicit as the officer escorted him from the dressing room.

"Well, we'd better go with him to ensure the record's set straight," Wilson said, ushering his colleague to follow the officer.

Before the two men left, Wilson paused, glaring at Artus and Franziska who remained frozen in the corner by the door.

"Don't think this is over yet," he threatened. "We will find and arrest her, too. It's only a matter of time."

Artus ground his teeth, his shoulders tensing, and Franziska quickly grabbed his arm.

"Let him go," she said to Artus before he could lunge at the detective as the spindly man disappeared after the officer and Timur. "We have to get Antoine. Now."

Deadman's Island.

Emma poked the dwindling fire with a stick. Anything to distract herself from Antoine's nervous mutterings as he paced circles around the caravan, parked and ready to be loaded up once the others returned from the show. Kizmet and Absinthe seemed content to watch him attempt to force a vision for the hundredth time. He desperately wanted to see what he could not, but the odds were not in his favour that evening.

"What does it *mean*? Tell me what this music means!" Antoine hissed, the fire sparking to life and illuminating his path as he marched around the corner of the vehicle for the umpteenth time.

Emma rolled her eyes and tossed the stick into the growing fire. She hadn't completed her last handstand for the day anyway. Franziska lived by the principle that everything could be solved by holding a good, long handstand. Why not? It was worth a shot.

She ambled her way to the edge of the forest, picking a sturdy birch for balance. Inhaling, she lifted her hands high above her head before diving forward.

Once her hands reached the ground she kicked her leg back. Her heels clinked against the rough bark, steadying her feet. She took deep, methodical breaths, ignoring the rush of blood to her head.

Her fingertips spread across the soft grass and pushed her toes off of the trunk, engaging her core. She swayed ever so slightly before finding her equilibrium. Closing her eyes, she focused on keeping everything as tight as possible like Franziska taught her to do as she counted down from sixty balancing in her handstand.

"Five... four..." she gasped, every inch of her body quivering as she reached the end of holding her tenth handstand for the day.

Although, with how long the night had drawn in she wasn't entirely certain it was the same day.

She dismounted, lowering one foot after the other as slowly and gracefully as she could muster. Though no one else could see her, she lifted her arms up with a flourish, fluttering her fingers.

"Brava!" A familiar hollow voice exclaimed from behind her.

She spun on her heel, smiling when her eyes fell upon the ghost, clapping his hands together as vigorously as if she could hear them. She was a little surprised that his hands even landed on each other without floating right through his palms.

His translucent body shimmered in the light of the fire. "You're an excellent acrobat."

"I'm still learning." She flushed.

"Who are you talking to?"

Emma jumped when Antoine suddenly appeared next to her, narrowing his eyes at the space in the grass next to her that Archie occupied.

"It's Archie Conray." Emma motioned towards the ghost as if Antoine could see him.

"Is this the ringleader?" Archie asked.

"Yes," she replied.

"Wow!" the ghost exclaimed.

Antoine flinched, covering his ears and Emma frowned at him.

"What's wrong?"

"It's this music that keeps playing. It's like… a tin flute. Can you hear it?"

"No," Archie and Emma said in unison, but only hers was heard.

"It grew louder just then." Antoine paced towards Archie, his ghostly body shimmering as he walked right through him.

"Is he always that strange?" Archie asked.

At the same moment, Antoine turned back to face Emma. "Did he say something just now?"

Emma nodded, eyes widening when she realised what Antoine was implying.

"Is he talking about me?" Archie asked.

"He's the music. This ghost you're speaking with." Antoine let out an airy laugh, scratching his head. "But how?"

The thump of hooves approaching pulled their attention from their discovery just as Kizmet let out a coarse grunt alerting them.

Three horses glimmered in the moonlight, two occupied by Franziska and Artus while the on that should've been Timur's was empty. The horses' wild mains flowed as they guided them to their camp. Antoine and Emma rushed to meet them just as they steered their galloping horses around the caravan.

Franziska and Antoine's silhouettes flickered in the light when they came to a halt near the campfire. Franziska's white hair fell over her shoulder when she dismounted. When she turned to face them, Emma knew instantly something was dreadfully wrong.

"Where's Timur?" Antoine asked, glancing between Franziska and Artus.

"He's been"—she covered her mouth, tears rimming her eyes. Antoine removed the space between them, taking her shaky hand and pulling her into a gentle embrace.

"He was arrested." Artus draped the reins loosely around a tree, brushing his hands before turning towards them. "That detective from London was at the show."

Absinthe let out a moan, following Kizmet to greet Artus. The leaves crinkled softly under their paws.

"Hello, my babies," Artus cooed, scratching them both behind their ears.

"How did this happen?" Antoine asked, giving his brother a hard look.

Artus looked up. "Don't be angry with me. Timur's the only one to blame for murdering all those people."

"He didn't do it!" Franziska cried, scowling at Artus.

"That's not what the evidence looks like," he shrugged, plopping down on a rock around the fire.

Emma blinked rapidly, her chin quivering as she held back tears of her own. How could this happen? He'd been so good and now he was feeding from the vein again? A chill swept over her that had nothing to do with the night's breeze. It was all her fault. If she hadn't said what she'd said, maybe this wouldn't have happened?

"The *evidence*?" Franziska pushed from Antoine, her livid eyes throwing daggers at him. "Is that more important than believing your family? You heard him, he said he didn't do it. Besides, that man's nephew was killed before we'd even arrived."

"Wait, who is she talking about?" Archie said, startling Emma.

She shook her head, barely able to reply.

"That's beside the point," Artus continued to bicker,

unaware of Archie's ghostly form hovering next to Emma. "Even you didn't believe him at first."

Franziska glared daggers at him. "You've never welcomed him, despite all the improvements he's made."

"All right, that's enough," Antoine shouted over the two, silencing their bickering. He rubbed his aching neck. "We must stop this. One of our own has been taken. You know the rules, Artus."

Artus's lip twitched but nodded his understanding. They were a family and a family always had each others' backs.

"Whose nephew are they talking about?" Archie prodded. "Would you ask them for me?"

Antoine cringed, covering his ears. "What's the ghost saying? Can he help us?"

"What ghost?" Artus and Franziska asked in unison, turning to face Emma.

"Uh, he wants to know whose nephew was killed." Emma folded her lips over her teeth, glancing at Archie whose body faded for a minute as a gust of wind nearly blew him away.

"It was a relative of the man who was with Detective Davies," Franziska replied, frowning when she followed Emma's gaze to the empty space next to her. "The boy's name was Archie."

"They're wrong." Archie gasped, making Antoine flinch, although what he heard Emma had no idea.

"What do you mean?" Emma asked, the rest of the circus leaning towards her as if that would allow them to hear the ghost's reply.

"I saw my murderer clearly before I died." Archie began to pace, his voice quickening. "Your friend, the vampire, didn't murder me."

"If he didn't, then *who*?"

"Who didn't?" Antoine asked, wringing his hands with impatience.

"He says Timur didn't do it," Emma replied.

"How can he be so sure?" Artus asked.

"I'd remember him anywhere." Archie gazed towards the forest, staring at nothing as his eyes widened.

Sensing his distress, Emma moved to stand closer to Archie. She rested a reassuring hand on his shoulders when a sudden energy sparked from her fingertips, shimmering in the darkness.

"Oh!" Franziska gasped, bringing a hand to her lips when Archie's translucent body flickered.

"Is that him?" Antoine asked.

"You can see me?" Archie looked between Emma and the rest of the circus members.

Emma removed her hand, straining the connection between them but Archie's ghostly form remained visible. "I didn't know I could do that."

"Well, if Timur didn't kill him then who did?" Artus cried, growing impatient.

"It was a younger man," Archie replied, his body fading. "Not much older than me and he had this… this scar. Under his eye. Couldn't forget it if I tried."

"Archie, if you weren't a ghost I could kiss you right now," Emma gasped, a sudden lightness in her chest as an idea popped in her head.

The boy flushed crimson, a sheepish grin spreading across his face as he wondered what they would be like.

"I've got a plan and I think it might just help you move on," she whispered to him before turning to address the rest of the circus. "I know how we can save Timur. It won't be easy but, with a little help from a ghost, it just might work."

16
A GHOST, A CIRCUS, & A TIN FLUTE

The City Gallows,
George Street & Lower Water

WILSON STEPPED OVER THE THRESHOLD, emerging on the top of the front stoop. The vicious wind whipped at his frock coat. The chill forced him to pull his scarf about his neck just a little tighter.

"Come along, Barnaby," Wilson said, taking a deep breath of the brisk air. "You're the only one who needs to be at this spectacle, anyway."

It was a messy ordeal in his business, the hangings and all. It was all a little too theatrical for his taste. Couldn't the punishment be far less ceremonial? Should he ever be put on trial, he'd hope to die like a true gentleman. With a glass of Dr Thorebourne's precious coca wine and a pistol. But then that was the point of it all, wasn't it? To die in disgrace for the misdeeds committed. And the crimes which this man today had committed were no small thing.

"Yes, yes, I'm coming," Barnaby said, shivering as he shut the door behind them.

The two detectives made the short trek down the sidewalk and onto George Street, following the growing throngs of men and women all headed for the morning's event at the city gallows.

"Such a glorious day, is it not?" Barnaby glanced up at Wilson, grinning from ear to ear as he waltzed beside him, an annoyingly chipper skip with each step.

"It's one I should want to miss, to be honest." Wilson struck a match, lighting up his pipe and greedily filling his lungs with its warmth.

"Oh come now, how can you not be happy on a day like this?" Barnaby chuckled to himself. "We've solved the case, and the vampire will soon be dead."

"He's not a—"

"Sorry, sir," a heavily cloaked young lad nearly ploughed right through him but quickly stepped out of their way just in time.

Wilson frowned, narrowing his eyes at the careless boy before turning back to Barnaby. "Honestly, I can't believe you're so quick to believe in something so ridiculous."

"If you'd only seen what I saw"—Barnaby shivered—"I know you'd believe in the supernatural. The murderer *is* a vampire."

"If he truly is a vampire," Wilson hissed, barely above a whisper, "then why do you think he was so easily caught? I would expect a vampire to have the ability to put up a good fight."

"Why does it matter?" Barnaby asked once they'd passed the marketplace directly across the street from the gallows. "He is and he didn't and now that he's caught, this shall be the end of my torment. I only hope that horrid flute I hear ends with it."

Wilson cocked an eyebrow. "But do vampires die after they're hanged?"

"It bloody well better die."

Wilson rolled his eyes, turning his focus to the wood platform standing tall on the shore's ledge. The crowd already began their mob-like banter, shouting and jeering one another. Some waved homemade signs begging for the abolishment of such a cruel punishment while others slung dirt and grime at them.

"I'm not sure we'll be able to reach the front without treading water," Wilson said, lifting his chin at the appalling display.

"Oh, good you're here," the arresting officer called from behind them.

They spun on their heels, facing the uniformed man.

"We won't be able to proceed without your statement." The officer nodded to Barnaby.

"Of course, that's why I'm here," Barnaby replied, pulling out his handkerchief just to be safe.

"Come along." The officer motioned for them to follow them towards the angry masses.

Wilson followed Barnaby and the officer, taking care not to make any unnecessary eye contact with anyone.

"Step aside!" the officer ordered, managing to part a barely walkable path up to the platform.

Barnaby gasped, gagging at the stench of sweat that enveloped them. It was almost too strong for even Wilson to endure, overcome with the strong desire to bathe in a sea of soap.

"Wait here." The officer motioned to the only free space next to the wooden steps that lead up to where a noose hung in the centre of the cross beam.

It was then the hairs stood up on the back of Wilson's neck.

He didn't know why, but he had an intense feeling that someone was staring at him. He frowned, scanning the crowd. Everyone in view was either preoccupied with throwing insults at each other or the barred cart nearing with the criminal.

"What is it?" Barnaby asked when Wilson hopped up onto the first step of the platform.

"I'm not sure," Wilson muttered, gazing out over the crowd. "It may be nothing."

The stout Mr Dods stood out immediately, standing on the far side of the platform. His grey sideburns sticking out underneath a faded bowler hat, exchanging a courteous greeting with Mr Talmage Sr who stood next to him, pristinely dressed from his embroidered black frock coat to his silk top hat. Their faces a matching picture of disgust having both lost a loved one to this treacherous killer.

But neither of them were paying him any attention, so Wilson dismissed both of them, moving his attention to the back of the crowd.

A head of bright red hair popped out to his left. A splash of colour in a large mass of brown and grey, but vanished just as quickly. A flicker of snow opposite the fiery red flickered out of the corner of his eye making him jerk his head to the right. Each time he thought he saw the members of the *Beaumont Bros. Circus* in his peripheral view, he was quickly proven wrong. What was going on?

"Off of the step, detective," the officer who'd escorted them bellowed, leading a group of police officers guiding the shackled prisoner towards his doom.

The burly man's head remained bowed, his hands tied behind his back and chains about his ankles. Even if Wilson didn't believe in the existence of vampires, the sheer size of the criminal made him second guess why he wasn't using his strength to put up a fight. But instead, he obediently moved forward to his death. The shackles rattled with each step, competing against the hollering crowd.

"On this day," an officer shouted, standing on the platform next to the killer and the hangman, gaining the crowd's attention as he read from the parchment he held. "Here to be hanged for the crimes of the murder of five innocent lives including our very own Mr Irvin Talmage Jr."

The crowd erupted in a storm of booing and hollering.

"How do you plead?" The officer looked to the shackled man who remained as still as a statue, his dark matted curls clinging to his face. He moved his gaze ever so subtly. Wilson almost missed the movement when the criminal caught his glance.

"Not guilty," his low, threatening rumble sent chills sweeping down Wilson's arm.

Yes, he was certain that something wasn't right. It was all too easy. He could feel it in his bones.

As if on cue, the melancholic tune of a tin flute swept by him for the briefest of moments. Was it even real? Or was it all in his head?

"Did you hear that?" Wilson asked.

Barnaby nodded, paling at the sound. "It's the flute. Something terrible is about to happen."

The air rustled their clothes, the air thickening as something invisible yet solid brushed passed Wilson's arm.

"Uncle Barnaby," a young voice whispered in the breeze.

"Ar-Archie?" Barnaby stuttered, spinning around trying to find the source of the voice.

But there was no one nearby who remotely paid them any attention.

"Where are you?" Barnaby cried.

Wilson grabbed him by the collar. "Are you completely inept? What if someone hears you like this? Besides, your nephew is dead. Where do you think he is?"

Barnaby shoved him off, straightening his sack coat. "How dare you—"

"Please, we don't have time for this."

The two jumped at the voice sweeping past their ear as if someone were running by them inches away.

"He's not..." the dull voice faded in and out. *"The killer."*

"What?" the two detectives asked in unison.

"That man isn't the killer..."

Wilson and Barnaby stood there, gaping at each other.

"That's impossible," Barnaby finally hissed. "He has to be the killer. The psychic told me, besides I *saw* him murder that woman in the streets."

"I saw who my killer was. That man they're about to hang... it's not him."

They looked up at the shackled man just as the officer pulled a noose over his neck. Barnaby's nervous stomach churned loudly.

"What should we do?" Sweat blanketed the lines creasing Barnaby's forehead.

"Do?" Wilson shook his head, looking away. "There's nothing that can be done."

"But what if we've got the wrong man?"

Wilson frowned. "You were so certain a minute ago. How do we know this… whatever this is not a trick?

"Uncle Barnaby, it's me. Your nephew, Archie," the urgency in the voice sent a gust of wind blowing past them, nipping at their top hats and coats. *"Remember the first case you wrote me about?"*

Barnaby gasped, blinking back the tears as he recalled their correspondence.

"The one you solved while on holiday in the Ottomans. You must remember..." the young voice pleaded. *"You sent me Turkish—"*

"Delight," Barnaby finished his sentence, eyes widening.

Wilson's heart raced, his mind reeling as the pieces fell into place. Turkish Delight. That was it. The reason it all felt too easy. It's because it *was*.

"How could I have missed this," he whispered, pacing back and forth next to the platform steps.

"Missed what?" Barnaby asked, but Wilson was too deep in thought to hear him.

The killer wasn't someone hiding in the shadows, they'd been in plain sight all along. Always there pulling at the strings, manipulating their every step. At Halifax Club when they'd been discussing the case, who had been there? And who had been available, whispering in Barnaby's ear? And in Mr Dods's ear?

He stopped, letting out an astonishing chuckle. "Oh, this is too good."

"What's too good?" Barnaby asked.

"I think I've now *actually* solved the case," Wilson shouted, gleefully bounding up the steps of the platform. "WAIT!"

The officer's head jerked towards him just as the snap of the trapdoor opening sent the man falling slack against the noose.

Screams mixed with jeers, but Wilson couldn't hear any of it over the blood pounding in his ears.

"No," he gasped, blinking rapidly.

The man grunted, struggling against the rope. Wilson lunged at the officer.

"What is this?" The officer cried, stepping back, but Wilson was much faster.

He snatched the officer's knife from his knife pouch. Spinning around, he used his momentum and sliced through the rope clean. The prisoner fell to the ground just as Barnaby reached the bottom of the platform, undoing his bindings.

"Run," he heard Barnaby order the man who didn't have to be told to comply.

The mob converged on the platform.

"Oy! What're ye think ye're doin?" Mr Dods cried above the rest.

The officer reached for Wilson, who quickly grabbed the man's hand, twisting it around and pinning it behind the officer's back.

"This man was innocent," Wilson growled, manoeuvring them so he could get a good look at the crowd. "And I've reason to believe the true killer is among us."

But where? He gazed between the throngs of people, taking advantage of the heightened vantage point, quickly profiling each individual and eliminating them.

A man at the corner of the square, cleaning his spectacles with his shirt. Wilson grimaced, wishing people would use some common decency and use a kerchief.

But he wasn't the killer and so Wilson moved on to the next.

"Stop that man!" Mr Talmage Sr shouted, pointing after the prisoner catching his escape in a peculiar caravan driving by on its way past the gallows and up toward Upper Water Street.

"You'd better be right about this," the officer growled, pushing himself away from Wilson, but Wilson wasn't paying any attention to him.

There, past the roaring crowd, leaning against the frame building just within sight of the platform, a familiar face stood out among the rest. Her wild hair billowed in the breeze like snakes, her hazy emerald eyes darkening when they met his.

"Madam Onay," he breathed.

She caught his eye, winking before covering her head with the hood of her cape and turning away and making a quick pace in the opposite direction further down Lower Water Street.

Wilson leapt from the stage, pushing his way around the mob. He had to stop her. It was his last chance.

Someone grabbed at his scarf, nearly choking up. Without hesitation, he spun around, unwinding himself and letting them have it as he pursued his prey.

"Not again," Barnaby sighed, ducking out from underneath the gallows after him.

He ran as fast as he could to catch up and the chase was on.

On the corner,

George & Lower Water Street.

Emma held her breath, rushing back to her post after getting her message to Timur about the caravan. She took care to remain just out of sight that the detective wouldn't notice her.

She exhaled once her feet met the sidewalk next to the marketplace and ducked behind a vacant vegetable cart. Everyone must've been at the gallows. A heavy fog curled around her ankles, and she beamed.

"It worked?" she asked, lowering her volume when a passerby glanced at her in confusion. To them, it was only a girl talking to herself behind a cart.

"Yes," Archie whispered as if others could hear him. "But I wasn't able to show them who. He disappeared and now they're chasing some woman."

"What?" she shrieked, peeking out from behind the cart just as Detective Davies and Archie's uncle sprinted down the street. "That wasn't supposed to happen."

"I know," Archie moaned.

"Come on. We have to help." She bounded down the sidewalk opposite the detectives, the cold biting into her lungs. She wasn't sure what she'd do once she caught them, she just knew she had to. To get them to arrest the true killer. The boy with the scar.

Out of the corner of her eye, she giggled at Archie pumping his arms and racing alongside her.

"Do you even need to move like that?"

Archie gave a sheepish grin. "Not really, but it is fun. Running's so much easier now."

They laughed together, enjoying their momentary distraction.

"Look." Archie pointed just as the two detectives and the woman vanished down an alleyway.

Emma nodded, slowing her pace. Her heart hammered against her chest, her breath forming clouds in the air as she slowed her inhalations.

They tiptoed to the edge of the warehouse framing the alley, smashing her back against the brick building and carefully sneaking a look around the corner.

She gasped. "Archie, you've got to see this."

"Wait, someone's coming!" Archie cried, tapping her on the shoulder leaving a damp mist in its wake.

She glanced over her shoulder, her throat catching when she spotted an officer emerge from around the corner. His head jerked up and down the street as if he'd lost sight of someone he was pursuing.

"What if he sees me?" She gasped, unable to pull in enough oxygen.

"Quick, hide in here." He motioned to a large bin next to them, removing the lid.

Her jaw fell open. "Archie, did you just *move* that?"

Archie glanced at the lid in his hand. It clattered to the ground as soon as he acknowledged what he'd done.

"Get down," he hissed.

She ducked behind the bin just as the officer neared, his brow wrinkled in confusion at the fallen lid. He glanced around, a mere inches from Archie, who held his breath.

Shouts echoed from the alleyway, pulling the officer's attention away from the noise before he could discover Emma crouched behind the bin.

17
ENDINGS & NEW BEGINNINGS

"HALT!" Wilson shouted at the woman just as she turned down the darkened passage, but of course, Madam Onay didn't heed his warning.

He motioned for Barnaby to follow him, pulling his pistol from a secret compartment within his frock coat.

Barnaby gasped. "Wherever did you get that?"

"A detective can never be too careful," Wilson whispered, moving his forefinger over his lips for him to be quiet.

Gripping the weapon, he ducked after their assailant into the darkness.

Madam Onay's footsteps echoed within the narrow space between the warehouses, slowing as she neared the dead end. The two detectives cornered her.

"There's nowhere to run, Madam Onay," Wilson called.

A bricked wall at the end of the alley brought her to a sudden halt. She glanced around, her hood falling as she tapped the walls. Wilson smirked. She was probably searching for a way out, but the only one way out for her and that was into custody.

"You've surrounded," Wilson called.

Madam Onay let out an ear-splitting scream, kicking a stack of bins that toppled over with a clatter. Her shriek melted into a cackling fit of laughter before she turned on them, slowly facing the approaching detectives.

Her emerald irises glowed in the shadows created by the little bits of light cascading over the rooftops high overhead. She sneered, their eyes locking. "All right, you caught me."

Wilson's lip twitched. "I should've caught you sooner."

Barnaby shook his head. "Wilson, it can't be her. We must have the wrong person."

"How could it not be her?" Wilson asked, continuing to aim the weapon at the centre of her forehead. "She was always out of sight, but because you confided in her she knew our every move. and could feed you and Mr Dods all of those lies about there being a vampire."

"But vampires *are* real. I saw it," Barnaby replied under his breath.

"Would you be quiet?" Wilson snapped and Barnaby jerked back. Wilson squeezed his eyes shut for a mere moment, regretting his knee-jerk reaction, but he had to push on. He had run out of his patience and couldn't understand why Barnaby was unable to grasp what Wilson thought so straightforward.

Wilson took a deep breath, his lock on the target never wavering. "It wasn't a vampire at all, was it, *Madam* Onay? If that's even your real name."

Madam Onay's throaty laugh sent chills down Wilson's spine.

"Look at the two of you, bickering like an old married couple," she hissed like a snake, taunting them as she sauntered towards them.

"Don't come any closer," Wilson warned, motioning for her to take a step back with the pistol's muzzle.

She raised her hands, a smirk upon her face as she came to a halt.

Barnaby scratched his head. "If it wasn't a vampire I saw killing that poor woman then what was it?"

"Isn't it obvious?" He cocked a brow. "It was all a lie. An elaborate scheme to make you see what you wanted to believe."

"No, I saw it. It was a vampire I swear." Barnaby's voice cracked as if struggling with his recollection of the facts.

"Don't be a fool, Barnaby, I went to the morgue without you. I inspected that woman's body. There were no markings at all, save for the gash in her neck and the knife in her hand that she used to slit her own throat with."

"But…" Barnaby blinked rapidly. "But I *saw* it."

"What you saw was what she wanted you to see. Isn't that right, Madam Onay?" Wilson focused his attention back on the petite frame of the psychic before them. "What I don't know is who your partner is and how he managed to get hundreds of ducks to all commit suicide while you murdered my friend's nephew?"

The woman remained silent, lifting her chin in superiority.

"Who are you working with?" Wilson's hand shook as rage boiled within him. "ANSWER ME!"

"You don't get it yet, do you?" She clucked her tongue, leaning her head to the side. "Such a pity. But you shall soon enough."

"What don't I get?" Wilson prodded.

Her arrogant laugh echoed between the buildings. "I don't work with anyone else because I don't *need* to."

Wilson scoffed. "You can't expect us to believe that. One person couldn't have killed Mrs Tilcott's cat and orchestrated the ducks while simultaneously on a boat far away. That's absurd."

"The only thing that's absurd is you thinking that little gun will do anything to me."

"I don't think it will." Wilson took a step forward. "I *know* it will now tell me who you're working with!"

"You know nothing." Her lip curled and her piercing eyes glared back. She didn't seem one bit fazed by the weapon. "But I want you to know, it will be fun watching you squirm as I rip your head off your skinny little neck!"

With sudden ferocity, she leapt towards them.

BANG!

Wilson blinked, pulling the trigger before he had a moment to process what was going on. The bullet hit her square in the chest, her mouth gaping as her body froze for mere moments before puffing into a mist of green and flesh-toned smoke.

"Bloody hell!" Barnaby cried, covering his ears with quivering hands.

Wilson couldn't move, his breath catching when the smoke that had once been Madam Onay churned and spiralled until it morphed into something else entirely.

"Where did she go?" He barely heard Barnaby over the sudden ringing in his ear.

It had to be a ruse. Some sort of smoke and mirror gimmick with a trapped door somewhere. He scanned the cobblestoned ground at their feet. There had to be a door or opening somewhere leading to an underground tunnel of some kind that would allow someone to appear to have vanished, but there was too much mist fogging up his vision.

He blinked repeatedly trying to clear his tearing eyes when a hand shot out through the sea of green mist before him and grabbed his wrist that still gripped the steaming gun. It had to be some sort of vaporised drug causing him to hallucinate because it all seemed so real.

A gust of wind sent his top hat leaping from his head, the

smoke suddenly solidifying around the arm. Before their eyes, Madam Onay transformed into a young lad. The black cape was replaced with torn trousers held up by suspenders. His dishevelled hair smashed underneath a ruddy cloth cap, his head bowed low. Inch by inch, he lifted his chin revealing, not the emerald eyes of Madam Onay, but the gleaming charcoal irises of a very different person.

"Hello, *detectives.*" A sneer spread across the familiar face, his eyes crinkling above a single scar.

Wilson gasped, realizing where he'd recognised him from. "It's you. The docker from when I first arrived, but… I-I've met you before."

"I thought you'd never recognise me." John Walsh's hand remained firm around Wilson's wrist, preventing Wilson from escape. "You're losing your touch, *Detective* Davies. I was so sure you'd figure out who I was long before."

A memory popped into Wilson's mind chills sweeping his arms. It was nearly midnight when a knock on his London townhouse brought the news of a strange murder. A young watchman had delivered the news, but it wasn't until now that he remembered the scar below the watchman's left eye. It was the same.

"You were the one who put me on the case with the butcher's daughter." Wilson drew in a sharp breath, his mind reeling. "But… *why?*"

John replied with a devilish smile, leaning in so his foul breath hit him hot on his cheek. "Don't you remember? How I got this scar?"

He tilted his head, allowing the light trickling down from above to highlight the jagged remains of an injury long since healed. A familiar sense of déjà vu swept through Wilson, sending chills down his spine. A distant echo trying to penetrate his secondary memory as it struggled to come forward into his primary. But no matter how many times he swept through his collection of facts and memories retained in his mind throughout time, it always ended with him running into a thick, black wall.

"Such a pity. But I remember you!" John spat in his face, bringing a crooked finger toward Wilson's cheek. The detective held his breath, recoiling as the lad's cold finger jabbed the soft skin below his eye. John's nail traced down Wilson's cheek, threatening to pierce the skin. "And I shall be the last face you see as you take your last breath."

Wilson scowled. "Then just *do* it."

Excitement flickered across the young man's dark eyes, his grip tightening. But then he stopped. "Not yet. That would be too easy for you, *detective*. And don't you want to play? After all, the chase is what you live for, isn't it?"

Wilson swallowed hard, hearing his own motto spoken to him sent his nerves on edge. He'd never uttered it to this fellow in his life. At least not that he could recall.

"You made it all too easy." John shoved Wilson against the brick building, pinning him and knocking the gun from his hand in the process. It fell with a clatter across the cobblestone. John waved his other hand at Barnaby when he tried to run away. A root climbed from between the paving stones, cracking the rock as it shot from the earth and snatched Barnaby's foot sending him toppling to the ground.

"Ooof!" Barnaby's jaw hit the rough ground.

"Barnaby!" Wilson cried, wrinkling his brow when his colleague remained still.

Was he injured? Would he survive? A knot formed in the pit of his stomach as he realised this was all his fault. If only he hadn't listened to that imaginary voice his drugged state had inspired. How long had John been poisoning them? Days? Weeks? Not a job for just a one-man-band that was for sure.

Wilson scanned the alleyway, searching for John's partner

or any sign of strings. There had to be some sort of contraption that caused his friend to keel over. But where was it?

John shoved him again, knocking his head on the wall. The world spun for a moment from the shock.

"I got inside your head, Davies." John let out a menacing laugh, his body shimmering as he shifted once more. His hair curled like worms, growing in length while his jaw and shoulders broadened. Suddenly he was no longer John Walsh, but Timur. "And now I'll never leave until you're dead."

"What trickery is this?" Wilson gasped, momentarily finding himself unable to move his legs.

"What '*trickery*'?" A younger man asked next to them.

Wilson jumped when a second hand grabbed his other wrist further restricting his movement. John Walsh stepped from behind Timur who had once been John who was also Madam Onay. His brain hurt.

"You… you were just…" Wilson opened and closed his mouth.

"I was just him?" John chuckled, an evil glint gleaming above his scarred cheek. He placed a hand on top of Timur's shoulder, suddenly vanishing in a puff of smoke that swept around the man who held him captive.

He squeezed his eyes shut, taking a deep breath and cursing himself for breathing in so much of that horrid smoke. It had to have contained more of the drug. But what drug could make him hallucinate such madness to the point that it felt so real? Nitrous Oxide? Or the vapour of a peyote cactus?

"This isn't real!" Wilson's voice shook. "I've been poisoned!"

"Don't you get it?" John's youthful voice spoke from within the form of Timur before he snapped his fingers, bursting into another mist of green until Wilson was staring back at a face he knew all too well. It was a perfect replica of his own, right down to his meticulously combed hair. "I'm anyone I want you to see."

Wilson ground his teeth. This was utter nonsense.

"Oh, I highly doubt that." Wilson pushed the form that looked like him off, suddenly returning back to John in a puff of smoke. "Once this drug wears off, there'll be a perfectly ordinary explanation for all of this."

John cocked a brow. "Will there be? Are you sure about that?"

Wilson shrugged his shoulders and dusted off his frock coat. He kept an eye on the gun now on the opposite side of the alleyway, calculating his chances of grabbing it before John. He wagered his odds were good. If John really did want to kill him, wouldn't he have done it by now?

"You're right, Wilson." John chuckled, twirling away from Wilson and leaping over Barnaby's still crumpled form on the ground. The poor man groaned, finally coming to. "I'm not going to kill you. Yet."

He grabbed Barnaby's collar before the detective could pick himself up.

Barnaby coughed. "Unhand me!"

"Please, there's no need for violence." Wilson lifted his hands, his foot staggering when he took a step closer to the gun. He had to push through whatever was messing with his mind.

"Of course not." John eyed the weapon meaningfully. He fluttered his fingers at the pistol and it shimmered instantly into a brick.

"Stop it," Wilson snapped, his eyes stinging from what must be the drug in the air forcing him to witness the impossible.

"Not. Yet." John spat. "Not until you've lost everything. Your career. Your friends. And your last hope of reality. Not until you stop denying what is. Then, and only then, will I make it stop."

With his free hand, John snapped his fingers sending Barnaby's body standing straight and tall, his arms glued to the side of his body. His feet peeled away from the ground and floated out of John's grasp.

Barnaby's eyes widened. "No, no, no! What's happening to me?"

Wilson gasped, blinking in disbelief as his colleague hovered in the air.

"It took only a few lives for me to get inside your friend's mind," John sneered. "To make him go mad enough to call on his friend, good old *Detective* Wilson Davies. How many more will have to die until you believe?"

He waved his hand and Barnaby arched over Wilson's head, plummeting into a pile of wooden crates lining the end of the alleyway.

"AHHHH!" Barnaby cried, groaning when he landed with a thud.

"NO!" Wilson ran to his friend's side. "Are you all right?"

"Your hell will end when you realise that magic is real." John's sing-songy voice echoed followed by a click of a pistol being cocked. "You'll learn that soon enough."

Barnaby and Wilson both looked to the entrance between the buildings as an officer stumbled into the alleyway. The breathless man held his gun firmly, aiming the muzzle of the loaded gun at John just as he was trying to make his escape.

"Stop right there!" The officer shouted at John who playfully lifted his hands.

"Don't get any closer!" Wilson warned the officer. "The air! He's poisoned the air with something!"

"It hasn't been drugged, silly." John's cackle was drowned by the officer's gunfire.

The bullet ricocheted past John down the alleyway.

Wilson ducked just in time, covering his head instinctively and squeezing his eyes shut. He held his breath.

Another shot echoed followed by shoes scuffling against the cobblestone. Wilson opened his eyes just in time to see John kick the gun from the officer's hand and sending a kick to his stomach. The officer crouched over, holding his aching stomach.

What officer would miss a shot from that close, anyway?

"He's getting away!" Wilson warned, pushing as much of the fog as he could from his mind and forced himself to stand.

The officer coughed, spewing onto the ground. A barrel rose up into the air high above John as he reached the entrance of the alleyway.

Wilson, about to stumble his way after him, froze. He blinked, rubbing his eyes. The drug must've been more potent than he thought.

The barrel tipped on its side, rolling over itself in the air until it suddenly dropped, falling on top of John sending the dishevelled young lad crashing to the floor.

"I'll take it from here." The officer winced, shoving the barrel aside and throwing a pair of handcuffs around John's wrists.

Wilson pursed his lips. "Of course."

Barnaby slowly rose to his feet, rubbing his chin. "Oh, thank heavens you're here, officer. This man attacked us! He's the killer you've been searching for. He admitted to it."

The officer looked to Wilson who gave a single nod.

"He's your man."

"Yeah, yeah, all right." The officer yanked John up onto his feet, the half-conscious lad groaning in the process, but stopped when he saw the giant hole and mass of dead root limbs strewn across the alley. The officer frowned. "What happened here?"

Wilson glanced around, hoping the drug had worn off, but there was no such luck. "Quick, you must get out of here before you become affected. I'll come to the station later."

"This is not the end! No, no, *detective*," John called, his lazy eyes seemingly going in and out of consciousness as the officer took him away. "It's only the beginning."

"It is for you," Wilson muttered, but they'd already rounded the corner and out of sight. He was certain John's accomplice was probably long gone by now, too. "Come along, Barnaby. Let's get out of here."

He hoped to wash the impossible things he'd just witnessed away with a stiff drink.

"Thank heavens for that barrel, otherwise he would've gotten away for sure," Barnaby said as they emerged from the alleyway. "But then how did it know to lift itself?"

Wilson frowned. "Don't be daft. We were drugged. What we saw could've been anything. It was probably the officer who lifted it."

"But John said he didn't drug the air."

"You honestly don't believe a mass murderer, to tell the truth, do you?" Wilson asked.

"But he survived your gunshot and sent me flying into the air with a snap of his fingers."

"It was all a trick." Wilson rubbed his brow in an attempt to ward off the headache that was rising in his prefrontal cortex. "He probably had his conspirator operating a contraption of some kind to make it seem as though you were flying when, in actuality, we were just dosed with a fair amount of a vaporised Lophophora cactus plant. That is all."

"But—" Barnaby began to protest when he suddenly stopped dead in his tracks.

Fog curled around the toppled bin, rising from the ground and forming a shadow. Glowing and shimmering, the outline of a young boy's face emerged. The ghostly shape faded in and out in the wind, nearly blowing the form away.

Barnaby squeezed his eyes shut for a second before opening them. "Archie?"

The ghost's jaw fell in unison with Wilson's.

"Uncle? You... you can see me?" The dull voice from the gallows returned. *"Wow, I can't believe it worked."*

A chill swept down Wilson's arms. It all seemed so real, but they must've still been under the effects of the hallucinogen. It was far more potent than he remembered the plant being. Perhaps John had enhanced it somehow? He would have to pay him a visit in his cell to find out about this and to draw out the name of his partner in crime.

"Yes, I can see you." Barnaby's voice cracked, his eyes tearing as he covered his mouth with his palm. "Wilson, look! It's my Archie!"

Barnaby ran to the translucent boy, reaching to pull him into a hug but stopped when his hand went right through him. "How... are you here? I saw you were dead?"

"I was dead. Still am, actually." Archie glanced down at his hands.

Wilson took a step around Barnaby, moving around the ghost looking for the mirror. It was highly improbable that Barnaby and he would both hallucinate the same thing. But, perhaps John's helper was still around here somewhere?

"He's here." Wilson spun around, eyeing every angle of the alley and the street entrance.

"Yes, Archie's here." Barnaby let out an astonished laugh.

"No, he's not. This is just a trick." Wilson waved at the imaginary boy hovering in the mist that, if tested, would certainly show a narcotic of some sort.

"It's not a trick," Archie replied, gaining Wilson's attention. *"But I did have some help."*

Archie looked behind him, meeting the gaze of a young

girl crouched underneath the building's wooden steps. She peeked around the corner, her crimson locks cascading over her shoulder sent the hairs on the back of Wilson's neck bristling.

"Emma," he snarled. "I should've known you'd be the one to help the murderer!"

He stormed towards her with every intention of taking the butcher's daughter straight to the police station.

"No, don't!" Archie shimmered his body, diving as graceful as a fish in the water at the detective. *"Emma's the reason you can see me. She has a gift, a magical gift and it's wonderful."*

Barnaby's hand grabbed Wilson just before he could get ahold of the girl. At the same moment, she shuffled out from underneath the steps and raced for freedom past the warehouses towards Lower Water Street. Her fiery man billowed behind her.

"You're letting her get away!" Wilson cried.

"Please, Wilson. Listen to my nephew."

"Don't be ridiculous!" He let out a guttural roar. "This can't be your nephew. Your nephew's dead and now you've let John's partner in crime escape us."

"Please, I don't have much time," Archie begged, gazing at both of the detectives. *"I wanted to thank you both. For letting that first vampire go. He was innocent, after all."*

"I told you he was a vampire." Barnaby grinned in victory.

Wilson rolled his eyes. "Have you never tried drugs recreationally? Seeing and talking to things that aren't there is to be expected."

Barnaby ignored all reason, of course, and continued to talk to what he thought was his nephew. To the world, Wilson was certain they both looked ridiculous. Out there in the streets, talking to an invisible fantasy.

"But I especially want to thank you, Uncle Barnaby." Archie

drew in a sharp breath. *"For your willingness to teach me the family business."*

"It's the least I could do, my dear boy," Barnaby replied, his smile melting as tears stung his eyes. "I'm so sorry. I should've been there for you. To save you. I should've—"

Wilson pushed against Barnaby's restraining grip, but he must've breathed far too much of the poisoned air as a dizzy spell came over him.

"It's okay. I've accepted that this was always my fate. To save an innocent life. I'm just thankful to Emma for giving me this chance to be seen one last time."

"For that, I shall always be indebted." Barnaby bit back a sob.

"I'm afraid this is goodbye, uncle," Archie whispered, his eyes glistening. *"Please don't worry about me."*

Barnaby nodded, so overcome with emotion he was unable to voice a response.

"I love you."

"I love you too, Archie." Barnaby squeezed his eyes shut, a single tear escaping and falling down his cheek.

The wind lapped at his lapel and dried the moisture upon his face. When he opened his eyes, the space next to the bin was empty, his nephew vanished and only the ache in his heart remained.

"We have to go after her!" Wilson mustered up enough energy to escape Barnaby's iron grip, but the circus girl had already disappeared.

"Please, let her be." Barnaby looked up at him, his eyes begging. "For Archie."

It took all of Wilson's self-control but, for Barnaby's sake, he remained where he was. He was far too lightheaded from the drug to run anyway. It wasn't the first time he pursued the redheaded circus freak and he was certain it wouldn't be his last.

"I daresay that circus may not be what I first suspected them to be, after all," Barnaby said, gazing down the street where the girl had vanished. "Whatever they are, they have my sincerest gratitude."

Wilson glowered. "They're murderers. I don't know how they set all of this up, but rest assured I will figure it out."

Barnaby shook his head, chuckling to himself. "I'm not one to disagree with your intuition, Wilson. But today, that young girl gave me the greatest gift. I think that deserves giving her a second chance."

Wilson huffed. "If you were so excited to be drugged, all you had to do was ask."

This is not the end... The memory of John's cackle made Wilson shiver. There was definitely something more to all of this, and he had an inkling it had everything to do with that memory he couldn't seem to unlock. He'd been set up from the start, he just didn't know how or why.

"Come, Wilson." Barnaby slapped him on the back. "I should think Tom has two gins waiting for us at the Two Crows. On the house."

Wilson's eyebrows drew together as Barnaby laughed at his secret joke, but didn't think to ask. His mind was too preoccupied replaying John Walsh's words in his mind.

I got inside your head, Davies... and now I'll never leave until you're dead!

Halifax Police Station

"ARE you sure you want to do this?" The officer asked, arching a brow. He held the metal key in front of the door, the only thing between Wilson and the cell block within.

The truth was, he wasn't sure at all. He knew there was a risk in addressing John Walsh alone, but what choice did he have? He needed answers, to find out where the others were. John had to be working with Emma, but there was no way a girl like her could provide John with a drug that potent. No, he had to have a third partner. Someone with medical expertise. Was it Dr Larson? Or someone at the military hospital? Surely, they wouldn't help a murderer. Would they?

Wilson straightened his back. "I'm sure."

The officer shrugged, inserting the key and turning it with a click. The door opened and echoed down the empty corridor, lined with a few entrances to cells with small barred windows and a latch at the bottom for inserting food trays.

"I'll be here," the officer replied, ushering Wilson inside.

He walked purposefully past the cell doors. A cough mingled with soft murmurs from the prisoners behind them. His shoes squeaked on the concrete floor when he came to a halt in front of the last door.

"You came to see me," John cooed, the sound grating on Wilson's nerves. The lad didn't even turn around to know that it was Wilson.

The detective balled his hands into fists, taking deep calming breaths before approaching the barred window.

John's small frame leaned against the cell wall, illuminated by the silver of light beaming from an obscured aperture near the ceiling.

"I knew you would."

"Where are the others?" Wilson asked, gritting his teeth for having to ask. He should've chased after Emma when he had the chance. "Who are you working with?"

John turned his head, peeking at him from behind his matted hair. The scar under his eye concealed by swollen black and blue blotches. "Does our sweet Barnaby know you're here?"

Wilson slammed his fist against the cold metal door. "Answer me!"

"I told you, *detective*. I work alone."

"You're lying," Wilson replied through barred teeth. "Tell me who provided you with the drug you poisoned the air with? Perhaps I'd be able to strike a deal with the constable?"

"I would never lie to you, my dear." John lifted a shaky hand towards Wilson from behind the cell door.

He instinctively took a step back but stopped. This was silly. John was behind locked doors and there was nothing to fear.

"The only poison is you," John hissed, extending his fingers out before balling them into a fist.

At that moment, a pressure surrounded Wilson's neck constricting his airflow. His mouth fell open, gapping for air. His hands flew to his neck, but there was nothing there. Blood rushed to his cheeks as he fought against the invisible force that strangled him.

"But rest assured, I'm exactly where I want to be." John uncurled his fingers and fluttered them, freeing Wilson who took in sharp breaths. He blinked, rubbing his neck as the oxygen returned to his lungs.

"You're a lunatic," Wilson coughed, shaking off the little specks that dotted his vision. He must've had some sort of attack. Perhaps the stress of it all was becoming too much for him. "But not to worry, we will find the others and they will all rot alongside you."

"The only one who will be rotting is you!"

Wilson grabbed his chest as it contracted. He had to get out of there before he fell ill right there in the cell block. He needed to regroup, but he was determined now more than ever to ensure John's stay in the Halifax police station was less than comfortable.

"You'll regret this." He glared back at John's gleaming charcoal eyes before turning to leave. He didn't know why he bothered. Had he truly expected to get a straight answer from him? If he sold out his partners then who would help him escape?

"The game is on, *Detective* Davies." John's menacing laugh followed him to the end of the corridor, making Wilson's skin crawl. "And it's your move next."

Wilson paused at the door, squeezing his eyes shut as he tried to steady the rage threatening to send him into a full stroke.

"Finished?" The officer asked, pressing his lips into a thin line. He must've heard every painful word of their exchange.

"For now. We will need to get answers about his accomplices," Wilson replied with a curt nod, noticing the cuts on his knuckles matching the prisoner's bruised eye. "And be sure you don't make it easy for him."

With that, he left the station behind him. Though the case infuriated him even more than the last one, at least this time one of the killers was finally behind bars. What more could he want in a day's work? Pulling on his gloves, he escaped the salty stagnant police station out into the crisp fresh air.

He paused on the front stoop, taking in the sun that glistened from high overhead, welcoming the tinge of warmth on his cheeks. The corner of his lips curled upward, the gravity of what he and Barnaby had accomplished setting in. Dr Thorebourne had been right after all. A holiday had been exactly what he needed, and the best of holidays it had been.

Deadman's Island

. . .

"It should be a little to the left," Franziska hollered at Antoine and Artus, supervising them as they worked to secure the Russian board on top of the caravan. She crossed her arms over her frilled blouse, her matching trousers glittering in the sunlight beaming over the tops of the spruce trees circling the disassembled campsite.

Though they'd grown rather fond of the island and their campsite, the circus as a collective had agreed. Unless something miraculous happened and Antoine foresaw them staying, it would be best to leave. Especially after what happened with Timur.

While Franziska and the Beaumont brothers worked to load up the caravan, Emma helped Timur in binding all of the tents.

"I'm sorry, you know," Emma whispered, tying the last knot around the tent. She glanced up at Timur who remained focused on his work. "I meant to say it before. Can you ever forgive me?"

After a moment, Timur looked up. Compassion reflected in his eyes. "It is already forgotten."

"How? I was so mean."

"No, not as mean as you might've thought. Besides, you were partly right." Timur picked up the bundled tent and slung it over his broad shoulder. "But that is what family is for. To remind each other to be brave."

A smile crept across her face. It was the first time he'd ever referred to her as family. She liked the sound of it.

Emma suddenly flinched when a twig snapped from the path leading into town. Everyone stopped what they were doing. Absinthe and Kizmet took their respective places next to Franziska and Emma for protection. Antoine reached for the revolver stashed in his belt. Timur looked to him for permission to inspect. Antoine gave him a single nod, and suddenly Timur vanished, using his supernatural speed to race after the source leaving a trail of dust and leaves in his wake.

A scream followed by a gust of wind echoed through the trees. Everyone held their breath.

Timur reappeared seconds later, carrying a short man in a brown suit and the brightest of pink waistcoats. His arms flailed as he tried to pry from the vampire's arms.

"Let me go!" the man cried.

Timur tossed him to the ground, the stout man's boots skidding on the uneven earth struggling to keep upright.

"I found this scum hiding in the woods," he growled, glaring daggers at the suited man.

"I wasn't hiding!" The man coughed, bending at the waist and resting his hands on his knees to catch his breath.

Though the colour drained from his face in fear, Franziska and Emma recognised him immediately.

"How *dare* you show your face here." Franziska spat on the ground at his feet, her ice-blue eyes growing wide.

"Wait." Antoine leapt from the roof of the caravan, landing next to Franziska. "Barnaby just wants to talk."

The man Antoine referred to as Barnaby glanced up at him, his jaw falling slack.

Franziska glared at Antoine, waving a slender hand at him. "Do you even know who this man is? What he's done?"

"Yes," Antoine replied, his features softening. "And he has something he'd like to say to all of us. Isn't that right?"

"But how?" Barnaby scratched the back of his head, an awed laugh escaping him. "I guess it doesn't matter how. I came here to extend my sincerest apologies."

He straightened, taking a moment to face each one of them in turn. Emma scooted closer to Kizmet, lacing her fingers in his comforting black coat.

"For myself and on behalf of my colleague, Detective Wilson Davies." He gave a small bow.

"And we're just supposed to believe you?" Franziska cried, her snow-white hair billowing about like a white Siberian lion's mane.

"I-I know you have no reason to believe me." Barnaby flushed, looking down at his feet before meeting Franziska's glare with pleading eyes. "But after what your daughter did for me… to have seen my nephew one last time…"

Tears stung the man's eyes, and he looked up to the sun. Emma looked to Franziska. They caught each other's gaze and, suddenly, Franziska's anger seemed to wash away, replaced with a sense of pride.

Barnaby cleared his throat, gaining their attention once more. "My Archie's found peace and I'm forever grateful to you." He nodded towards Emma.

A warmth radiated through her, the feeling of helping someone sending her heart aflutter.

"But more importantly, I'm sorry to you," Barnaby continued, turning to Timur who stood, frozen behind him. They locked eyes, sharing an exchange of understanding before he turned back to the group. "And not to worry. Your secret is safe with me."

Antoine stepped forward. "And what of Detective Davies? He's been searching for our Emma to arrest her."

"Yes, he has, hasn't he?" Barnaby nodded, pressing his lips into a thin line. "But he'll come round. If not, I'll make sure to keep him out of your way."

Emma's eyes widened, a sigh of relief escaping her. Would this mean they wouldn't have to run after all? Was she free after all?

"Thank you," Antoine said, extending a slender hand out to Barnaby who shook it firmly. "It means the world that we are now at peace."

Barnaby stepped back, turning to leave when he glanced at their half-packed caravan. "Are you leaving?"

Antoine raised an eyebrow, his eyes glazing over as if he were staring into the future.

"Yes," Franziska replied just as Artus let out a whistle, gaining the panthers' attention.

"Come on, let's finish this up," Artus called.

"Well, I hope you'll reconsider…" Barnaby breathed as an expression between fear and wonderment spread across his face when the panthers complied. He shook his head, snapping out of his daze. "I should think this city could use a little bit of magic, and I'd love to see you perform one last time."

He shrugged, waving his farewell before leaving to go back down the path he came. Antoine's eyes returned to focus just as Barnaby disappeared around the bend.

"It appears you are free, Emma," Antoine said.

"Yes!" she exclaimed, flinging her arms up.

The group laughed as they watched her dance in place. Emma wasn't sure where they were going next or if they would stay, but right then and there she was certain she was the happiest she'd ever been. No longer did she have to live on the run for fear of being taken away from her only family. And maybe, just maybe, she'd finally be able to perform. The energy from her rising mood sent her skin glowing like the sun, a tingling sensation spreading throughout her body.

Pop. Pop. Bang!

Showers of light sprung from her fingertips, soaring towards the heavens before popping in a sea of colour. They had no idea what tomorrow would bring, but there, under a blanket of gold, pink, and silver fireworks, the circus danced in celebration.

It was just a little thing, but to Emma, it meant the world. What a dull life it would be if one did not take the time to celebrate the small victories in life. Though the future would prove it had much more strife and struggle in store for the *Beaumont Bros. Circus,* at that moment, everything seemed right in the world. And so they took this opportunity to embrace each other, to laugh, and be merry. As imperfect as a family could be, they would always have each other and these moments that brought them together.

CONTINUE THE SERIES

www.TabiSlick.com/TheYuletideKiller

JOIN THE UNIVERSE

Paranormal* | *Historical* | *Urban Fantasy

Join my monthly reader's group to stay up to date on all of my new releases, giveaways, book news, and receive personal updates from behind the scenes of my writing strategies.

www.TabiSlick.com/Join

MORE TO DISCOVER

GASLAMP FANTASY & MYSTERY

The Detective's Nightmare

The Yuletide Killer

DARK URBAN FANTASY

Tompkin's School (A Supernatural Academy Trilogy Book 1)

Tompkin's School (A Supernatural Academy Trilogy Book 2)

Tompkin's School (A Supernatural Academy Trilogy Book 3)

CLEAN PARANORMAL ROMANCE

Timur's Escape

For more on the books of the Transitioned Universe visit the OFFICIAL website at www.TabiSlick.com

ACKNOWLEDGMENTS

I owe a huge thank you to my beta readers and review group. Your expertise, advice, and criticism challenge me and my writing is a thousand times better for it.

To the authors who've inspired me throughout the years, including, but most certainly not limited to, Arthur Conan Doyle, Robert Ludlum, and Kiersten White.

To my friends and family who've always believed in me even when I didn't. You mean the world to me and I thank you for your support and for rooting for me.

I also want to give a shout out to Hans Zimmer and his scores from the Sherlock Holmes soundtrack which I listened to on repeat throughout writing this novel. Your music is legendary.

In addition to Zimmer's skilful compositions, it would be a shame not to also call out the violinist and composer, Aleksey Igudesman, who perfectly encapsulates the tone and essence of the infamous detective.

For those aforementioned and to you for reading, I owe you all a huge thank you from my heart to yours.

www.ingramcontent.com/pod-product-compliance
Lightning Source LLC
Chambersburg PA
CBHW030334310726
48979CB00001B/27
9781734556872